QUEEROES

Save the Gay...Save theWorld

QUEEROES

Save the Gay...Save theWorld

Steven Bereznai

LETHE PRESS
MAPLE SHADE, NJ

Published by Lethe Press, 118 Heritage Avenue, Maple Shade, NJ 08052.

www.lethepressbooks.com   lethepress@aol.com

First printed in Canada by Jambor Publishing, 2009

First U.S. edition, Lethe Press, 2010

Cover & Layout by Dan Bowers

ISBN 1-59021-215-0   ISBN-13   978-1-59021-215-8

For Lance Lamore.
We have shared many adventures.
You are my Queero.

Special thanks to Dan Bowers, Anthony Collins,
Geoff Jones, Joshua Marans, and Michael Rowe.

Chapter 1

Dear Diary,

You had totally better be sitting down for this because you are NOT going to believe what happened after school today...

Troy Allstar worked at the jewel in the crown of teen life in the small town of Nuffim. He was a junior seller at the Aberbombie and Stitch store at the Nuffim Mall. To look at him, one would be hard pressed to find someone with a better look for a clothing line known for its black and white posters of athletic young men, in various stages of undress, tossing footballs in idyllic fields or flicking towels at each other after a hard game and a hot shower.

The Nuffim High senior was strategically packaged in blue jeans and a tight-fitting Aberbombie and Stitch T-shirt that had his fellow jocks saying "Dude, how do I get arms like that?" and made girls trance out as they stared at him. His physique had a similar effect on 99.9 per cent of the guys in the drama club—including the teacher.

In short, Troy looked like the kind of white-bread, carefully coiffed guy who got whatever he wanted. But what he got today, as he folded shirts with military precision, was everything he did *not* want—starting with the appearance of his former best friend.

"Hey," a deep voice said.

Troy looked up from a pink T-shirt bearing the label "1932." He stared into the face of a handsome black youth in an A&S outfit that complemented his own. The guy's name was Jesse. He had strong cheekbones, a shaved head, and a bod to rival Troy's. Together, they really were an Aberbombie ad come to life.

"I thought you quit," Troy said.

The delivery was cool, calm and nonchalant, just like everything else about Troy. Outbursts were for the weak, and he was one of the strong.

"Change of heart," Jesse replied, pinning his name tag into place above his bulging chest. For all his muscle, he moved with a surprising grace—he'd been a gymnast before his growth spurt years ago. He glided past Troy, easing up to a pair of teen girls checking out jeans. Within moments Jesse had them off to the change room to try on the roughed-up denim, along with belts they hadn't even noticed before.

Troy felt a flush rise to his cheeks as he stared at Jesse, at the curve of his back, the gleam of his scalp, and the sensitive spot of the neck that ran in between. He choked the feeling down.

Control your thoughts and you control your feelings. Control your feelings, and you're in control, Troy preached to himself. A second later he was like a stone inside. But this evening had only just begun to test the emotionally tight-fisted Troy Allstar. He cracked open a bottle of Etienne water, and drank it down to relieve the sudden parching in his mouth.

With every swallow he became the first teen in the town of Nuffim to find himself, and his destiny, forever changed.

The Aberbombie store sat on a raised platform in the middle of the Nuffim Mall, like a throne overlooking throngs of teen royalty and social paupers alike. It had a clear view of the movie theatre, with its posters of big-budget sci-fi fests and lowbrow Will Ferrell comedies. But the best entertainment was taking place in real time. There was pretty boy Markham and the hulking Riley, tossing popcorn at each other, oblivious to the fake butter they were getting on their letterman jackets. The two jocks were Nuffim High's quintessential alpha males, maintaining their status by humiliating any lesser being they came across.

"Hey, check it out," Markham said, tapping his goon with the knuckles of one hand and pointing in the direction of the Goodwill store.

A stupid grin creased Riley's pug face.

Emerging from the thrift shop was none other than Liza "Lezzie" Larsdon. It was Markham who'd given her the moniker back in grade school, just as he'd christened every geek and outcast he'd ever encountered. Liza's height had reminded him of a lesbian pulp novel he'd found at his aunt's house years ago. He never forgot the giant Amazonian princess on the cover. Of course, that temptress had been a proud warrior, whereas Liza's shoulders hunched and she mumbled more than spoke.

Moving with the speed of crack commandos, Markham and Riley grabbed straws from a nearby dispenser and chewed on bits of paper napkin, using the saliva-soaked balls to load up their weapon of choice.

Liza turned in their direction and actually walked towards them, her eyes to the ground, oblivious to the danger. She was like a dodo: destined for extinction. She finally looked up and saw the straws pointed at her. Fight or flight ought to have kicked in, but she'd developed a different survival strategy long ago—that of a turtle retreating into its shell. She froze up as the first round of spitballs hit her cheek.

Markham and Riley laughed and reloaded. Their second volley smacked her forehead, the third targeted her large breasts concealed in a frumpy gray top, while the fourth, fifth, and sixth barrages got caught in her long, scraggly black hair. Still she didn't move, didn't say anything, didn't react. She just took it, until the pair of jocks grew bored with her lack of reaction.

"Later, Lezzie," Markham said as they tossed their straws at her, then to Riley he said, "Let's razz the Dungeons & Dragons nerds."

As they left, Liza's frozen innards slowly thawed. She felt the anger in her clenched fists. *They are such goddamn assholes!* she wanted to shout, but the thought was replaced by another: *I hate myself!* Her throat clenched around the self-loathing in her rising bile. And deep in the roiling pit of her diaphragm, she latched onto a vision of hope, and spoke it aloud.

"You'll get yours."

She drank back a bottle of Etienne water, unaware of what it would do to her, or the path it would take her on.

Ducking around a sparkling fountain in the middle of the mall, Markham and Riley ignored Liza glaring at their backs. They'd found fresh prey, and were closing in on the store affectionately named Games and Geeks. It was the anti-Aberbombie, in every way imaginable.

The display windows were full of painted figurines of warriors battling dragons, futuristic armies squaring off against one another, and comic book heroes in dramatic poses and skin-tight costumes. Instead of Aberbombie's muted tones and soft lighting, the interior of the store was under a merciless fluorescent glare, and its customers were the polar opposite of A&S's tanned and built gods and goddesses. Here were to be found sallow complexions, braces with headgear, and questionable personal grooming.

Gibbie Allstar felt right at home. He was Troy's younger brother, though as Gibbie rolled an octagonal die onto a board with several starships on it, one would hardly think the two had a single gene in common. Where Troy appeared corn-fed, Gibbie looked like a corn stalk. Troy's square jaw and wrestler's body gave him the air of Hercules. Gibbie's head was too big for his body, and in Grade 4, Markham had nicknamed him Newt. The name stuck.

The long history of torment heaped on Gibbie by Markham and Riley in the years that followed ran like a clichéd checklist: hallway noogies, ruthless locker lock-ups, and classic head-in-the-toilet torture.

"Your antimatter is mine!" Gibbie cried to his chubby friend Matt and their gaming buddy Carl, a twitchy Asian kid whose words smacked with saliva whenever he spoke.

A small TV set played the nightly news as Gibbie triumphed.

"And we have breaking news this hour," the announcer read. "Etienne bottled water is being pulled from the shelves, after reports of a contaminant getting into the supply at the local Calebraton bottling plant..."

Gibbie looked at his unopened bottle of Etienne water and tossed it in the garbage. He wiped a strand of greasy red hair from his eyes and got ready to roll again, until Carl grabbed his wrist.

"What's the matter?" Gibbie asked.

"Red alert!" Carl hissed, his mouth drowning in spit.

Gibbie spotted Markham and Riley from afar, and the geek's eyes grew wider behind his Coke-bottle lenses.

"Dude, you better..."

Matt did not even have to finish the sentence. Gibbie ducked behind the counter just in time for Markham and Riley to saunter in. The owner of the shop, a dwarf of a man with a gut and a goatee, puffed himself up as he waddled aggressively towards the two intruders.

"I told you two not to come in here anymore!" he blubbered, his face turning cherry red.

"Simmer down, Lardy," Markham mocked, his sharp features scanning the small store for their favorite victim. His high cheekbones twisted in disappointment when he failed to spot Gibbie. He had to settle for flipping the playing board in front of Carl and Matt, sending their cards, dice, and ships rattling to the floor.

"Ooops," he said. "Sorry about that."

In the reflection of the TV, Gibbie watched Markham step on the board, making it crunch under his sneaker, before walking towards the counter. A commercial featuring Popeye eating spinach flickered on the TV. Markham leaned forward, reaching a muscular arm for a figurine of Superman that sat atop the set. If the bully looked down he'd stare right into Gibbie's four eyes staring up at him. A bead of sweat ran down the youngster's nose.

"Do not touch that or I'll break your hand, I swear to God," shouted the fat store owner. He held a baseball bat menacingly.

"Chill, man," Markham snorted, hands held up in peace. "It's all good."

Gibbie held his breath. Markham leaned forward again, and callously knocked Superman over. It fell right onto Gibbie's chest. Gibbie and the Man of Steel stared eye to eye. The shopkeeper charged. Markham's laughter sounded like a snorting pig as he pushed Riley out ahead of him, giving the store owner the middle finger as the two sprinted away.

Still, Gibbie didn't move. His entire body was like a coiled spring and he was afraid if he budged he'd snap apart. Slowly he calmed his racing heart and cautiously lifted his head above the counter.

"Are they gone?" he asked, trying to keep the shaking out of his voice.

"Clear!" Matt said.

"You've got to stand up to them," the shop owner advised.

"Yeah, and get the crap kicked out of me," the scrawny boy muttered, coming to join his friends, who were putting the board and pieces back on the fold-out table.

If Gibbie had left it at that, the rest of his high-school life would have continued in much the same vein—go to school, get harassed, do homework, then come here to play role-playing games. But like every geek worth the name, Gibbie was a dreamer, and not just because he was into elves and Captain Kirk. His biggest fantasy went beyond Tolkien and Roddenberry; it was flesh and blood, and at this very moment, it walked by.

The beautiful blond cheerleader of Gibbie Allstar's dreams.

Immediately Markham and Riley were forgotten. The world moved in a slow-motion swirl of golden locks. They cascaded from side to side as this cheerleading beauty's head swung seductively. In Gibbie's mind, Bonnie Raitt sang "Something to Talk About" just for him, adding to the soundtrack of his life and drowning out breaking news reports of the Etienne bottled water recall.

"Oh boy," Matt said, spotting the reason behind the spaced-out look on his buddy's face.

"Not again." Carl's words swished in his own spit.

Gibbie stepped towards the door.

"Don't do it," Matt urged, grabbing his friend. "It's not worth it. Markham and Riley could still be out there!"

"I have to," Gibbie replied. He spoke as if in a trance, not even looking at his friends or the board game he was abandoning. His muse was before him, glowing with an inner light. Gibbie knew if he could boldly go where no Gibbie Allstar had gone before, if he could cross that final frontier and explore the strange new worlds beyond, his life could be different. *He* would be different.

On impulse, he went for it.

Chad "I'm here, I'm queer, OMG! *Gossip Girl's* on!" Lenwick traipsed through the mall with his best friend, Mandy Kim—or, as he liked to call her, Mandy Candy. Most adults would think these two high-school seniors were boyfriend and girlfriend. Their response to such assumptions was a flat-out "ew" and "I can do better."

Their kids would've been stunning, though.

Chad got away with calling her his Asian princess. She had a slender build, small perky breasts, and a poise honed by years of dance classes. Mandy called him her ho—short for homo, but also because she claimed he dressed like a hooker. It had taken since freshman year for Chad to shape his body into a physique, and he was determined to show off his hard-earned muscles in the tightest FCUK jeans he could find. But despite his beefcake bod, there was no confusing him for an Aberbombie jock. His nails were too polished, his skin too tan, and his gait was just too darn gay.

He was checking his cellphone for text messages and, with a sigh, shoved it in his man purse.

"No word from Jake?" Mandy asked as they strolled past a KitchenAid display, each of them taking delicate spoonfuls from their cups of non-fat frozen yogurt.

"Whatever," Chad said dismissively. "He's in college now, and who cares about a closet-case football meathead?"

"You do," she replied, which she could tell was not what he wanted to hear. So to distract him she added, "What about that one?"

She gestured her pink spoon in the direction of a college student sitting with some buddies, eating Big Macs.

Chad shrugged, unimpressed.

"What?" she demanded. "His face is cute."

"And his shirt is concealing," Chad replied, scraping out the last remains of his frozen yogurt, "Look at the shoulder-to-waist ratio and you'll see exactly where his McHappy Meal is setting up fat camp."

"You're good," she acknowledged.

"It's a gift," he shrugged.

They were playing their favorite game: Find Me My Future Husband. They tossed their empty yogurt cups into the trash and cracked open their bottles of Etienne water. Each drank thirstily, but when Mandy screwed the cap back onto her bottled water, she noticed something amiss.

She stared at her palm, and then held it up towards Chad. "Does this look right to you?"

He gazed at her wriggling fingers.

"Yeah, it's your hand, girl," he scoffed. And yet for just a second Chad could've sworn her digits looked translucent.

"Come on, babe," he said, his tone softer, "I think we both need a Diet Coke. Our aspartame levels must be getting low."

He slid her arm into his, which *really* made it look like they were honeys.

"Do you ever wish..." she began, her words trailing off.

"Wish what?" he pressed.

"It's just, we put all this effort into this," she made a sweeping gesture to her body, "and sometimes it feels like it's all the wrong guys who notice, you know?"

"You mean like him?"

They stopped near the Aberbombie and Stitch clothing store and stared at their classmate, Troy Allstar. He was fastidiously arranging a display of cardigans.

"Do you regret dumping him?" Chad asked.

She shook her head. "He kisses the way he folds shirts: with precision. First you press your lips together, then you squeeze the other person's lips, then you insert your tongue. It was like someone handed him a point-by-point manual on how to make out, and he'd follow it to the letter. If you ask me, that's why he got passed up for captain of the football team. He plays the same way. With precision, not passion."

"Too bad," Chad said, " 'cause he's got himself a wicked body."

"Maybe *you* should date him," Mandy snorted.

"Maybe I will," Chad winked.

"Can you imagine!" she laughed.

For just a second, Chad could, but he thought it best to keep that to himself. Being out was one thing; going after his best friend's straight ex was another.

"You know," Chad observed, "If you hadn't dated Troy, then maybe Jesse..."

"Do *not* say it," Mandy hissed.

"They were best friends," Chad chided. "Did you really think you could date one and then the other?"

"I still can't believe Jesse turned this down." Again she gestured at her body. It was then that Chad noticed Jesse in the store. Great. There was Troy, Mandy's old squeeze, and there was Jesse, Mandy's current obsession. *This has 9/11 written all over it*, he thought. Before Mandy could spot Jesse, Chad led her towards the food court. He tossed his empty Etienne water bottle into the recycling.

It was then Chad began to feel different. He swore he could smell two of the most annoying cheerleaders on their squad coming their way.

Lacey and Stacey, he thought, without turning around.

"Lacey and Stacey," Mandy called out, standing on tiptoes and waving over Chad's head.

"Not a word about Jesse," Mandy muttered under her breath, and with a grin she clapped enthusiastically. "Hey, hotties!"

"Hey!" the two girls squealed, running up to them, shopping bags bouncing as they hugged Mandy tightly.

From the scrunched-up look on Mandy's face, Chad knew she just wanted to push them away. They were vacuous to the point of making Mandy and Chad appear deep. He prepared to play the old "I think I have diarrhea—Mandy, can you drive me home?" card, but from the corner of his eye he caught sight of his own reflection, and what he saw made his heart beat quickly.

His eyes...there was something messed up about his eyes.

"I...I have to go pee," he said.

"I'll come with," Mandy offered.

"No!" Chad said hastily, shielding his face with his hand and darting away from the trio.

Out of sight, he hid behind a giant fern and pulled out a My Little Kitty compact. He stared into the mirror. Instead of his beautiful blue eyes, he gazed at a pair of pupils in the shape of vertical slits, surrounded by a yellow iris.

"This is effed up," he said, trying not to panic.

There was a light tap on his shoulder, making him shriek. He whipped around, and when he saw who it was, he restrained from hitting him.

"Gibbie!"

"Hey," the gawky redhead replied, fidgeting from foot to foot. "Funny running into you at the mall."

"Sure," Chad said. "Listen, do I look weird to you?"

Gibbie's eyes were huge behind his thick glasses. His gaze drank in Chad's strong thighs, tiny waist, and rounded pecs, barely contained in a Nuffim High cheerleader zippy.

"You look awesome."

"Nothing...off?"

"*Really* awesome."

Chad looked back into the mirror. His eyes were normal again. Still, things were not as they were. A kid dropped a small bouncy ball and Chad flipped in the air, diving after it instinctively. He caught it in his mouth and landed on his hands and feet.

The kid, his mom, and Gibbie all stared. Chad bashfully removed the ball from his mouth, wiped off the saliva and returned it to the little boy. His mom grabbed it away from him and threw it in the garbage with a disgusted look on her face. Chad was uncharacteristically speechless.

"So where you headed tonight?" Gibbie asked, as if nothing untoward had just happened. It was as if he was on autopilot, and was not deviating from his assigned trajectory no matter what.

Meeting Gibbie's four eyes, Chad growled, "I'm going hunting."

The little nerd blinked uncertainly, and Chad had to shake himself as if from an altered state.

"I mean, I need to get home, that's all," Chad said. And he really did. He did *not* feel right, and what the heck was up with catching a ball in his mouth? That was gay, even by his standards.

"Well maybe we could, I don't know, I mean later, if you're free..." Gibbie stammered.

His stuttering words trailed off, and then stopped altogether. Riley and Markham were coming out of the Fitness Depot carrying tubs of protein powder. Their faces widened into smiles as their eyes fell on Gibbie.

"What were you saying?" Chad asked, staring at his nails and wondering why they were so long when he'd just cut them.

Gibbie's mind went blank.

"I gotta go," Gibbie said quickly. The thought of being humiliated was bad enough, but in front of Chad? It was too much to bear. Already the two jocks were bearing down on them. Chad's nose twitched at their scent, but he was in no mood for the likes of them. He needed to run free.

"See ya at school, squirt," Chad said, tousling the younger boy's hair, not even noticing how greasy it was.

Chad headed for the revolving doors separating him from the parking lot, and the wilderness beyond.

Gibbie swallowed hard and backed away from the approaching jocks.

Chapter 2

Troy Allstar watched the whole thing go down. Gibbie and Chad had been standing not far from the Aberbombie and Stitch store while Troy finished folding waffle-patterned undershirts with the A&S logo sewn onto the chest.

Troy had long suspected Gibbie was a homo, *and* that he had the hugest crush on Chad. But there was no time to dwell on it. Troy's boss saw to that.

The guy was an MBA student eager to work his way up to Aberbombie corporate. His name was Joe, but he made everyone call him Diesel. It was more Aberbombie, he explained. In fact, Diesel looked like he'd stepped right out of the catalogue, with his A&S Mountain low-rise jeans, chunky hand-knit Savannah sweater, and the perfect mix of shoulders, cheekbones, and laser-whitened teeth.

"We need to talk," Diesel said in a way that did not bode well, "Listen, you fold shirts like nobody's business, but when it comes to sales…well, you're no Jesse, that's for sure."

Jesse was ringing up a cute brunette's purchase of a tank top and miniskirt. She waved at him as she left and he flashed her his patented smile.

Diesel kept his tone on the level, almost pained, but Troy felt something else. Relief perhaps, that it had finally been said.

"Look, man, sales is about emotion, and connecting with your customer, and it's like you've got this wall up all the time."

Because I do, Troy wanted to reply.

"I can get better," Troy objected, "I…I can emotionally connect with people."

Diesel seemed to be considering it when he noticed someone coming through the store's doors. It was Troy's brother, Gibbie. His face was flushed and he kept looking nervously over his shoulder. Markham and Riley were closing in.

"I'll tell you what," Diesel said, "Sell that kid something, and I'll think about it. Just remember, there are different kinds of shoppers. Moms looking to get a present for their kids want to seem cool. Those jocks over there"—he pointed to Markham and Riley—"want to feel like they're part of the tribe, and this one"—Diesel took in Gibbie's skinny frame and thick glasses—"he obviously doesn't belong here, but you have to make him *feel* like he could. This kid is a wannabe. He's got a dream, to be like one of us, and we sell that dream for $45.99 a T-shirt."

It would take more than a shirt to make Gibbie fit into this world. He looked around uneasily, and not just because he was about to have his ass kicked. Dance remixes of rock classics blared, a wooden canoe hung from the ceiling, and all around were framed prints of muscular tween guys dressed in soaked jeans snapping towels at each other. Gibbie stopped next to a beaten-up metal sign with a cartoon of a smiling fish that said, "Throw back undersized catches."

Diesel gripped Troy by the back of his shoulders and pushed the teen forward.

"Make a sale," the manager hissed.

"Hey, Tr—" Gibbie began.

"Hello there, customer!" Troy said to his brother, jerking his head meaningfully towards his boss. "Now this would look swell on you!"

He held up a shirt that said "SWIM TEAM."

Gibbie looked back at Riley and Markham, who had stopped just inside the store. Markham mouthed the words "You're dead" while making a slitting motion across his neck.

"Come on," Troy said, angling his brother towards the change room, "I'll deal with them, but you've got to try this on."

Diesel gave the thumbs-up as the pair passed by.

When Gibbie emerged from the change cubicle, the XS shirt hung loosely about his frame. Troy could sense his brother now felt ridiculous *and* terrified. "Are they gone?" he asked fearfully.

"One size smaller, coming up," Troy said as Diesel poked his head in. Seeing Gibbie's uncertainty, Troy added under his breath, "I'll check, all right?"

Back in the showroom, Troy pulled out an XXS. He searched for Markham and Riley, but thankfully they were gone. Chasing off potential customers to defend his brother would not have cut it for Diesel.

"Here, these are for those two guys in the change room," Diesel said, handing Troy a belt and a hat. "They've got up-sell written all over them."

"What two guys in the change room?" Troy asked, his stomach sinking as he began to suspect where Riley and Markham had gone.

"Oh, and get them to try our new cologne," Diesel added as Troy was already running back towards his helpless younger brother.

Gibbie stood silently berating himself as he waited for Troy to get back.

Today I had to ask Chad out. It just had to be today. What is wrong with me? I knew Riley and Markham were out there. Did I actually think getting rejected by Chad was worth it? I am such a loser! I deserve to get beaten up!

But then he remembered something. Chad tousled his hair.

He touched me!

Gibbie gently patted his own skull, remembering the feel of the blond's palm on his scalp. It was sheer bliss.

That's when Markham and Riley stepped into the changing area. They towered over Gibbie's trembling form.

"Look who it is," Markham taunted with feigned surprise. "Little Gibbie Allstar actually thinks he's cool enough to wear Aberbombie. Is that it, Gibbie? You think you're cool?"

"N-n-n-n-o," he stuttered, looking about desperately for Troy.

"Oh, so you think you're hot," Markham concluded.

"I d-d-d-d-don't think I'm hot," Gibbie protested, his cheeks burning red.

"Yeah, I think you do. Maybe we should cool him down," Markham said. Riley's laugh always came out as a bark.

"We've got a very special beverage for you, Gibson," Markham said, and already Riley was pulling out a bottle of Etienne water from a knapsack.

"That was recalled," Gibbie protested. "I heard it on TV, just twenty minutes ago. There was some sort of contamination at the bottling plant."

"Yeah," Markham agreed, "I heard that too. I was going to save this for you and your nerd buddies at school tomorrow, but since you're here…"

He cracked the bottle open and Riley grabbed the small teen in his paws.

"Please," Gibbie begged. "I have irritable bowel syndrome. That could really mess me up…"

But Markham was already wedging the tip of the bottle into Gibbie's mouth, shoving it deep between his cheeks. The smaller boy tried to pull away, but Riley gripped his jaw, forcing him to swallow or choke. Down, down the water went, and when the bottle was empty Markham let it clatter to the floor.

"There," Markham said, "*Now* you're cool."

Gibbie was panting and wiping away tears. Markham pulled out his iPhone.

"I have got to get this onto YouTube."

"No!" Gibbie shouted, reaching for the jock's arm. He couldn't let Chad see him like this. He wouldn't! Markham's free hand swung back and came flying down, aimed at smacking Gibbie's cheek, like so many times in the past. Markham never hit hard enough to leave a mark—just enough to hurt, and more importantly, to humiliate.

But this time, somehow, somewhere, someone rewrote the script. For just an instant it was as if the scene was caught in freeze-frame. Not one of them moved. The shock ran that deep. Skinny, useless little Gibbie had caught muscular Markham's wrist, and held it fast.

The larger teen tried jerking free. Gibbie waited for his grip to break easily under the force of Markham's superior arm. It didn't happen.

He's playing you, Gibbie told himself.

The guffaw from Riley confirmed it.

So why did Markham look so freaked out? Why was he grimacing in pain?

"You...you're hurting me," Markham squealed, his voice hitting an unfamiliar pitch. "Let go, you little faggot!"

Understanding crept slowly into the young nerd's mind.

As if in a dream, he shoved Markham, and the force sent the teen flying off the ground in an arc, smashing into the far wall. Troy skidded into the changing area just as the jock crumpled to the ground. The wrestler stared in amazement at the dented drywall.

The hulking Riley tried punching Gibbie and the scrawny geek caught the bully's fist in his palm. With a jerk of the arm, Gibbie sent the giant through the air to land on top of Markham. They lay there, stunned for a moment. They clambered to their feet, gazing at Gibbie in awe. The little nerd took a menacing step towards them, and they ran out of the store.

"What the hell just happened?!" Diesel demanded, poking his head around the corner and screaming at Troy. "You're supposed to be up-selling to those two, not scaring them off!"

Anybody else would've panicked, but Troy was Troy.

"Shoplifters," was all he said.

Diesel's eyes widened and he darted away, screaming for security.

With the store manager gone, Troy turned to his little brother.

"Did that just happen?"

Judging by Troy's tone, he could've been talking about the weather. Any surprise or concern he might have expressed were locked in quarantine. Gibbie stared at the busted-up wall, nodding slowly.

"So," Gibbie said, panting and wiping nervous sweat from his brow.

"So," Troy agreed, still trying to process.

"Are you going to tell on me?" Gibbie finally asked, staring at the dented wall. He did *not* want to get into trouble.

Troy pondered this. Who would he tell? What would he say? And who would believe him? More importantly, this was his baby bro.

"I don't think so," Troy replied, "but…"

Carefully his rational mind began bending the situation this way and that, leisurely printing off questions in his mind like a clunky dot matrix. Slow was good in times like this; slow kept the panic at bay.

"Are you on something?" Troy asked

"No!" Gibbie replied, and Troy *knew* his brother was telling the truth. He wasn't sure how he knew, but he did. Pinpricks were running down his spine, and as if they were some sort of polygraph test, he had no doubt about his brother's honesty.

"Go home," Troy said.

"And then?" Gibbie asked.

"And then," Troy paused, thinking, rearranging his thoughts like a never-ending game of Tetrus. "And then we're going to pump some iron."

Mandy was vowing revenge on Chad, who'd left her stuck with Lacey and Stacey. Of course Mandy had no idea that her best bud was going through a metamorphosis more traumatic than coming out and puberty combined, and so she thought, *You are so dead, my fag friend.*

"I wish I had a homo," Lacey sighed to Mandy as Chad disappeared from sight.

"You're so lucky to have a gay," Stacey chimed. "It's, like, better than

Prada."

"Gay rights!" Lacey and Stacey cheered, giggling and clapping each other's hands. Their jaws never stopped chomping on their gum.

I'm so tired of being public property, Mandy thought. *I wish I could just hide.*

Fortunately, a side act was only a few feet away. If Mandy was going to be forced to perform, she always felt better using a prop. And there was the perfect target—their large-boned Amazonian classmate Liza Larsdon.

Liza stared into the window of an outdoors store. On display were a range of crossbows, hunting knives, and even a bear trap. She looked down at a piece of paper in her hand. On it, in her delicate calligraphy, were the words "Hit List."

"Oh my God, is that Lezzie Liza?" Mandy said loudly, forcing her voice to a titter. She took a look at Liza's bulky gray top and sweatpants. She might as well have been wearing a muumuu.

Girl, why do you have to make this so easy? Mandy wondered, almost feeling sorry for the gentle brute. Sometimes it was like clubbing a baby seal. A giant baby seal in stretchy pants, but a baby seal nonetheless. These thoughts she kept to herself. Aloud, she said, "Honey, Addition Elle's that way."

She was about to touch Lacey and Stacey on the back while they were distracted by their own laughter, and say to them, "See you later girls," so she could go grab Chad by the scruff of the neck and make him pay for abandoning her, but before Mandy could execute her plan...

"I love what you've done with your hair!" Lacey cooed to Liza, picking out one of the spitballs Markham had shot there.

"But it seems to be missing something," Stacey added.

They both reached into their mouths and removed their pink bubble gum.

Mandy's eyes widened in horror; a little verbal abuse was one thing—they were in high school after all—but there was a line, and it was about to be crossed.

"Guys, that's really not cool," she began to say.

But her words were futile, her reach too short. She watched as if in slow motion as Lacey and Stacey stuck their gum in Liza's hair.

"Much better!" the two girls squeaked with delight. "Hubba Bubba chic!"

Lacey and Stacey covered their mouths as they squealed in glee. Mandy looked about in quiet embarrassment, knowing full well she'd started this, and had done little to stop it.

"Liza, I'm sorry," she began, but there was something in her classmate's face that halted Mandy's words. The look in "gentle" Liza's eyes reminded Mandy of Hannibal Lecter, the bone-chilling cannibal from *Silence of the Lambs*.

Oh my god, she's going to punch me! Mandy realized in horror.

Mandy prepared to defend herself against Liza's ogreish fists, but the giant of a girl did not clench her fingers. Nor did she break the camping store's window and reach for a hunting knife. Instead Liza went for Mandy's weapon of choice: words that struck more surely than a bludgeon.

If one were to ask Liza why she snapped at this moment, instead of all the other instances of her awkward adolescence, she'd probably shrug and grunt, "I dunno." But the truth was she did know. She felt a new strength within herself, and it demanded to come out.

"I am not going to take your shit anymore, you goddamn fake-and-bake whores!" she shouted.

The words rumbled up and grew somehow, a deafening roar that made Liza's entire body shake, and drowned out the drone of the mall's Muzak. The reverberations went beyond a bellow, cannonballing up from Liza's chest, and the world trembled at her fury.

Mandy, Lacey and Stacey's eyes opened wide and, for just a second, the latter two wore a "Who do you think you are?" look on their pretty faces—until they saw the concussive blast issuing from Liza's mouth, a rippling haze that curdled the floors and walls in its path.

Store windows shattered in a spray of glass, floor tiles buckled and snapped, chairs and tables in the food court were ripped from their moorings while neon signs burst with electric sparks.

The cheerleaders were tossed—not like the Barbies they patterned themselves after—but like rag dolls; their limp bodies buffeted and bounced. Stacey slammed into a column. Lacey sailed through the air and bashed into a salad bar.

Mandy was a different story.

While the food court had suddenly turned into the tornado scene from *The Wizard of Oz*, Mandy's body did not move. She held her arms up protectively, and stared through the space between them at a flickering shield of what appeared to be static electricity. It stood between her and Liza. Tiles shattered against it. A bench bounced off. Even the girl's roar seemed muted.

Liza clamped her mouth shut and slammed her hands over her lips. Silence and an eerie stillness reigned. Her concussive blast died and she gazed in horror at the destruction all around her. Mandy could tell that Liza had no more clue this would happen than the rest of them. But what exactly had happened, and what was that strange shield holding Mandy safe?

Water streamed from pipes that used to be attached to taps. There was a loud bang and popcorn shot everywhere. A life-sized statue of a clown teetered, and then crashed to the ground, fracturing its face in two.

Mandy took sharp, quick breaths. The shield that had protected her from Liza's voice fizzled and disappeared.

The two girls stared at each other. Loud shouts came from the other end of the mall. The teens' eyes snapped in that direction. Frantic footsteps echoed closer. Liza's gaze grew wider. She kept one hand on her mouth. The other pointed at Mandy in horror.

"What are you doing? Stop pointing at me!" Mandy shrieked.

Liza's finger remained locked on her. The tall girl's entire arm shook, making jabbing motions in the air towards Mandy. The cheerleader looked down at herself, and watched her own chest slowly disappear.

"Holy Hannah Montana," she swore.

Mandy lifted her hand and watched as it, too, faded away. She turned to a storefront mirror, and before her eyes, her body slowly seemed to dissolve.

The last thing to go was her lips.

Suspended there, glossy and red, they wailed, "But I'm too pretty to die!"

Chapter 3

Troy sat astride his bicycle in the Nuffim Mall parking lot. It was full of police cars, ambulances, and fire trucks. Red emergency lights flashed across his brow.

"You okay, son?" a cop asked him.

"Yeah," Troy lied.

The truth was he felt dizzy, and a cold sweat ran down his back.

A few feet over, another cop was questioning Jesse.

"Can you tell me what happened?" the police officer asked.

"There was a scream," Troy said, "and, I'm not sure, an explosion?"

Troy rubbed his temples.

"You sure you're okay, kiddo?" the cop pressed, gripping Troy's shoulder.

Kiddo—that's what Troy's dad would call him. The memory made him smile, and for a moment the needles scraping along the inside of his skull softened into gentle fingertips.

A CNN chopper buzzed overhead and a slew of flashes from reporters' cameras went off in Troy's face.

His classmates Lacey and Stacey were being loaded into ambulances. Both were unconscious and would wake with no clear memory of what had transpired. The media would write it up as an explosion, the cause under investigation. And then there was Liza. She was the kind of girl everyone, including Troy, overlooked, and yet today something about her drew Troy's notice. A paramedic was putting a bandage over a scratch on her temple. She looked about nervously, as if expecting to be put in cuffs. The needles in Troy's brain returned as prickles of guilt. Troy shook it off. His imagination was getting the better of him.

"Okay, kiddo, you're clear to go," the cop said.

Jesse came over to Troy.

"You want a ride?" Jesse asked, holding up his motorcycle keys.

"I'm good," Troy replied, indicating his bike.

Jesse shrugged indifferently, but the needles in Troy's temples were back again, and he felt his former friend's disappointment. Jesse zipped up his leather motorbike jacket and climbed onto his Apache. Troy watched him disappear into the night. The needles in his skull receded, and for a moment he found himself wishing his former best friend would come back.

Troy shook his head. He had to get away from all this insanity. He had to be careful getting out of the parking lot, but once he was free of police cars and ambulances, he began pedaling as hard as he could, reveling in the feeling of air on his skin, and the pleasant burn of his legs as he pumped the pedals of his bike harder and harder. He was free of his boss, free of Jesse, free to just be.

He crested a hill, and stopped. His heart hammered, and at first he assumed it was just from biking so hard. But looking around, at the forest on either side of him, he felt a strange, disembodied excitement. He squinted into the darkness. He was alone on the road; at least he appeared to be. All the same, he couldn't shake the feeling that he was being watched. He could hear the gurgling of the Nuffim River beyond the trees flanking him. Several streetlights were burned out, leaving the street more in shadow than light. It was the perfect scenario for a slasher flick.

"Hello?" Troy called. "Jesse?"

He shook his head and was about to resume biking home, but from amidst the foliage Troy spotted a pair of bright yellow eyes staring at him.

For a moment he thought it was a wolf. Troy's chest heaved up and down. He could sense the owner of the yellow eyes bunching up its muscles.

"Oh sh—"

The thing with the yellow eyes burst from the brush, knocking Troy sideways. It landed on the road, sprang forward, and disappeared into the woods on the other side of the road. The only thing Troy really saw was its tan skin over hard muscles, clothed simply in a pair of pink underwear—American Apparel, if he wasn't mistaken. All the same, Troy knew...

Sensed exactly who it was.

Troy got up and onto his bike.

He stared after the creature—*Chad*—that had knocked him over. He was gone from sight, but Troy could feel the cheerleader still. Gibbie was not the only one who was somehow changed this night. Chad's wildness exuded from him in waves, slamming Troy's heart and making it hammer. It filled him more surely than the rush of a wrestling match. This was insane; this was more insane than Gibbie throwing Markham and Riley. This even went beyond the mall being hit by a localized earthquake, or explosion, or whatever the heck it was. Troy had kept it together through all that. He'd quarantined his feelings when Jesse had offered him a ride on his motorbike. But enough was enough. Whatever wildness brimmed within Chad, Troy could feel it too, and it ran through him like a drug.

"This is totally crazy," he said.

And that made him smile, 'cause Troy Allstar was ready to be crazy's bitch.

"Game on," he said, and he began pedaling in pursuit.

Chad ran, hard and fast. At times on his two feet; at other times he'd find himself loping along on all fours. He didn't know why he'd charged Troy, and now a gust of wind brushed past, carrying the wrestler's scent.

Beyond the trees, Chad saw a bike light keeping pace on the road.

He's following me!

Up ahead, the forest thinned out. Lights flickered from the many windows and street lamps of the subdivision up ahead. The cheerleader ran faster, bursting out of the bush, right in front of Troy. There was a skid of tires. He would've only caught a momentary glimpse, Chad assured himself, launching himself easily over a fence, into a backyard, through more backyards, over a front gate, onto the street, across it, into another yard.

The wind brought a gust of Troy's scent nearby.

How?

Faster, Chad ran, in the opposite direction from his own house, then into an abandoned lot. It was there he doubled back, clambering over a dumpster, ducking behind the Nuffim Community Center, skittering around its outdoor pool, hurling himself upwards off the diving board, over onto a neighbor's deck, and then scaling down a tree trunk, easy as pumpkin pie at a Thanksgiving feast.

Lost him, he smiled.

Home was in sight. He ran faster, reaching the house, jumping onto the sagging porch with its cracked pots of dead flowers, reaching for the chipped front door, grinning as he yanked it.

The fox beats the hound, he gloated inwardly.

The door remained shut.

He pulled several more times.

The deadbolt clattered, stubbornly locked.

Chad searched for his key, but while he'd managed to keep his underwear on, he'd stripped his pants long ago. A gust of wind carried another whiff of Troy. The rattle of a bike chain grew louder.

Chad looked down at his hands. Claws sprouted from where his manicured nails ought to be. In the reflection of the mailbox he could see his face. It was him, with his pretty lips and defined cheekbones, but at the same time it wasn't him. His eyes—they were all messed up again, looking like a cat's, and his ears, pierced twice on the left side ("Left is right, and right is wrong!" Mandy had advised him at the piercing studio), now ended in pointed tips, as if he were a companion of Frodo Baggins.

"Jesus H.," Chad cursed, tears coming to his yellow eyes, "what's happening to me?"

He couldn't let Troy see him like this. Chad looked about desperately. Bars protected all the first-floor windows—a legacy of his mother. She never had adjusted to small-town life before she died. Looking up, Chad saw his bedroom window open, the curtain blowing in and out.

It had been an odd chase—and chase was exactly what it had been, Troy quickly realized. Chad was attempting to lose him, and the harder Chad tried, the stronger his desperation became, and the easier it was for Troy to follow him. It beamed like a beacon in the night.

But it ended here.

Troy watched a silhouette climb up the sheer wall of a two-storey house...

Like a squirrel.

...and disappear within an open window.

Chad let his body drop to the floor with a thud. He waited for his dad to call out, but all lay silent.

Of course, he realized. It was two-cent wing night.

He opened his bathroom door and flicked on the light. In the mirror he saw again what he'd become: the teeth, claws, eyes, and ears. It wasn't just a trick of the night. This was real.

More tears glimmered in his yellow pupils.

"What's happening to me?" he blubbered.

"Chad?" a voice called from outside.

He looked back to the window in alarm. He ran over and slammed it shut, pulling the curtains fast.

"Chad!" Troy called again, his voice now muffled by the closed window. Chad opened it for a moment.

"Just a minute!" he yelled, and then slammed the window shut again. He ran back to the bathroom. He still looked like a freak. His desperation grew. He squeezed his eyes shut and flexed every muscle in his body, fists clenched tight.

"Change back, change back, change back...," he growled.

He opened his eyes, panting. He still looked like a monster.

He made a little mewling sound, his face a grimace of frustration. He pulled his hair back, a gesture he usually reserved for when he contemplated what he'd look like with a facelift, but today all he wanted was his old face back.

His heart was hammering so hard it was almost all he could feel.

"Keep your cool, Lenwick, just keep your..."

And that's when it occurred to him. If he could just calm down, then maybe he'd return to normal.

He ran to his dad's bedroom. One half of the double-sink counter was littered with razors, men's deodorant, a worn toothbrush, and a tube of toothpaste squeezed from the middle. The other sink was completely clear. He opened the mirrored cupboard above the clean side. Inside was bottle upon bottle of prescription medication, all with his mom's name on them.

He grabbed a bottle labeled Valium. Troy started banging on the front door and it made the blond boy start. He popped open the lid and took a handful of pills, swallowing with a gush of water from the tap. Staring into the mirror, Chad breathed heavily, waiting for it to work. Nothing happened.

"Damn it!"

The banging on the door was louder this time.

"Coming!" he yelled.

He opened the medicine cabinet again, searching. He grabbed a bottle of what he thought was an anti-anxiety medication, and took another handful of pills. He waited. Still his eyes glowed yellow, the pupils vertical slits. He reached for a third bottle. He got the lid open, but when he tried emptying pills into his palm, they scattered all about the floor.

He tried to focus on them, but his vision grew blurry. He felt himself teetering. He stepped back to right himself but instead found his legs giving way beneath him. His claws scrambled at the countertop to hold himself up, but they had no strength, leaving behind long scratch marks as he slid downwards. He knocked over another plastic bottle and pills pelted him.

"Help," he whimpered in a final panic as darkness descended upon him.

Troy started banging louder on the door, then slamming his shoulder into it.

"Chad!" he yelled. Needles tickled Troy's nape, and he could feel his classmate slipping away.

"What the hell have you done to yourself?" Troy wondered out loud.

Pull it together, he ordered himself, *Chad's dying*. Troy could feel it. With force of will, he pushed the emotions into a box.

He pulled futilely on the window bars. Clambering up the drainpipe resulted in a broken drainpipe. His grip failed as he tried scaling the brick wall.

"Think," he ordered himself. He could call the fire department. They could break down the door, but if they did, what exactly would they find? Something was happening in the town of Nuffim, and the cheerleader was among those affected. Who could say what they'd do with him?

He's dying, he reasoned. *What difference does it make?*

A vision of a cage came to his mind. It made a big difference.

"Think, Allstar, think!"

In a fit of inspiration, the answer came. He pulled out his cellphone. Ignoring the slew of messages on it, he called home. When he heard the voice on the other end, he spoke in a panic.

"Gibbie, it's Troy. There's an emergency."

Chapter 4

Gibbie sat in the basement of the Allstar residence. Above him there was a flurry of heavy footsteps, and a lot of picking up and putting down the phone. He paid it no mind. He had to concentrate. He stared at Troy's weight set. The bench press was loaded with heavy discs on either end of a barbell.

"No problem," he said, pushing his thick glasses up his nose.

He lay on the bench, gripped the bar and grunted loudly. With a final "hur-huh!" he shoved upwards. To his dismay, the bar remained rooted in place, not budging an inch. He pressed again, grunting louder this time. Once more, it remained unmoved. A third time he tried, growling and twisting his torso back and forth. The weight practically yawned in boredom.

Gibbie sat up.

"Better start with a warm-up," he reasoned. He went over to Troy's set of dumbbells, neatly arranged on a rack, and by turning scarlet in his cheeks, holding his breath, and putting everything he had into it, his two hands managed to move a single sixty-pound dumbbell from its spot.

It immediately slipped from his grip and he had to jump back to keep his toes from getting squished as it cracked the cement floor. He panted, staring at the fallen weight. To the right was a cable machine. He went to it, grasped the metal rod hanging from it, and pulled downwards.

It moved with complete ease.

"Yes!" Gibbie cheered in victory.

He looked back. The pin had fallen out of the stack of weights, and all he'd done was lift five pounds. It was already starting to feel heavy in his grasp. He lowered it with a clang. The poster of a flexing and tanned body-building champ looked down on him mockingly from the wall. Gibbie's shoulders hunched in defeat.

The commotion upstairs grew more frenzied and there came a clomping of feet down the basement stairs.

"Gibbie, you haven't seen your brother, have you?" his dad asked from the middle of the steps.

"No," he replied.

"Your mother and I are going to drive over to the mall. There's been some sort of explosion. He's not answering his phone. You stay here in case he calls, okay?"

"Yeah," Gibbie said, feeling a surge of worry.

His father went back upstairs, the front door slammed shut, and there was a *vroom* sound as the car started up and pulled out of the driveway. The phone in the kitchen began to ring and Gibbie ran up to get it.

Troy's voice came from the other end in a rush.

"Gibbie, it's Troy. There's an emergency."

"Are you okay?" Gibbie cut in.

"I'm fine, now listen…"

"Mom and Dad are freaking out. Where are you?"

"I'm at…"

Troy looked around, stepping closer to the street sign.

"McDougall. I'm at 15 McDougall Street. Gibbie, you have to get here, fast. Someone's in trouble."

"Well, call 9-1-1."

Troy barely heard.

"Just get here. I need you to bust down the door or rip off the window bars."

Gibbie didn't say anything. Flashes of trying to lift the weights—and failing—passed through his head.

"Gibbie, are you there?" Troy asked.

"Yeah," he said.

Troy kept looking around. There was a garden gnome with a broken nose standing by a dead tree on the lawn.

"I know this place."

Gibbie rubbed between his eyes. He paced.

"Troy, I can't help you."

"Gibbie! Just get your scrawny ass over here."

"I'm hanging up," he said. "You better get home before Mom and Dad…"

"Coach Lenwick lives here," Troy cut him off, speaking more to himself than Gibbie.

The jock had been here for several team barbecues, back before he quit football to focus on wrestling—and to put some distance between him and Jesse. It was strange how, even now, it was so easy to forget that the coach was Chad's dad. During those barbecues, Chad had been nowhere to be seen.

"Gibbie, are you there?" Troy panted. Troy tried once more tugging at the bars covering the front window.

"Coach Lenwick," Gibbie whispered. He always remembered who the coach's son was. "Chad."

Gibbie dropped the phone and ran down the front steps two at a time.

In moments he was on his bike, its rusty chain squeaking with every turn of the tires. Chad's face rose in his mind, and he pedaled harder. Troy's panicked voice echoed in his ears. Gibbie pedaled harder still. At first it was slow-going, Gibbie's panting filling the night. But as he approached a hill, wind began rushing through his hair. The houses to either side became a blur. His breath caught on a faintly acrid odor.

Staring down at the pedals he watched bits of smoke rise up from the gears.

He crested the hill and zoomed past a stop sign. He caught up to a car ahead of him. Now he was alongside it. The driver—old Bill from the post office—looked at Gibbie and gave a nod of the head. Whatever über-strength he'd lost in his arms, his legs had gone supersonic.

A sharp rattle made Gibbie gaze down just as screws popped loose from his bike frame and its gears went flying apart from the stress of such a high speed. His bike careened into the ditch, with him alongside it. When old Bill jerked his head back towards Gibbie, all he saw were rows of houses, leaving the old fellow thinking he'd imagined the youngster pedaling as fast as a car.

Gibbie pulled himself out of the dirt and stared down the street.

"Chad," he whispered, and began to run.

It started as a light jog. Normally the little geek would be panting after a few steps, reaching for his asthma puffer, but, much like riding the bike, he instead found his pace increasing. He looked down at his legs in amazement and then, staring back up along the street of tidy houses, he ran faster. The clunking of his rubber soles against the pavement grew into a steady *swish, swish*, his shoes barely touching the ground as he propelled himself forward. He flew several feet with every stride. Wind whipped his hair. Street lamps grew blurry.

Smoke rose from the treads of his shoes, just as it had from his bike, and his nose was filled with the smell of burning rubber and asphalt. Faster and faster he ran—not quite a speeding bullet, but quicker than any other creature alive.

Gibbie stuck his foot out to make himself stop at Chad's street, and wound up tripping. He toppled to the sidewalk, rolling over and over, ripping his shirt, and landing on his stomach. He lay there, winded.

"Goddamn it," he cursed with his first breath. Yesterday he'd been a knob. Today he was a knob with super strength.

Then he remembered Chad.

Little Gibbie was up and running seconds later, careful to slow his pace as he caught sight of Troy in front of No. 15. Gibbie skidded to a halt, only now realizing that his brother might ask him how he knew where to go so readily.

Google Maps, he told himself. *Just say Google Maps.* It wasn't stalking until there was a restraining order.

But Troy didn't ask. His voice was unflinching as he pointed at the front door.

"Break it down."

Gibbie opened his mouth to protest, to explain that despite his Flash-like arrival, his strength had been useless earlier. But before a word could come out, he was awash with a desire to please, and obey.

He ran at the door with all he had.

The door splintered like the thinnest plywood as Gibbie's body came hurtling through. Hinges went flying and the doorknob embedded itself into the wall.

Troy nodded in approval. "Nice," he said, and ran upstairs.

He followed the fading trail of emotion, ending in Coach Lenwick's washroom. On the linoleum floor was a facsimile of Nuffim High's male cheerleader and token fag, except...

"We have to call an ambulance," Gibbie said.

"No," Troy said. He got on his knees and cradled Chad's head. "Look."

He felt the whiff of jealousy from Gibbie, and Troy knew in an instant that his thin little brother would've given anything to be holding the muscular teen. Troy gently pushed the awareness away.

One thing at a time.

Chad's eyelids twitched, open but unseeing. His pupils looked like a cat's. His ears were pointed, like a character out of *Lord of the Rings.* His teeth were sharp points. He had fangs and claws.

"It's not a costume," Troy said.

"He's different, like me!" Gibbie exclaimed.

The excitement that radiated from him tugged at Troy. It was so full of desperate yearning. *Now we can be together,* it practically cried.

"Different," Troy echoed. *Like us.*

Pills were scattered all over the floor, and empty pill bottles. Impossible to know exactly what he'd taken or how much. Troy slapped Chad's cheek a few times, and his classmate gurgled and twisted pathetically in his lap.

"I could hold him," Gibbie offered, "if it would help."

"I've got him," Troy replied.

He wasn't sure why he was denying Gibbie his wish. Gibbie's crush was faintly creepy under the circumstances, but perhaps it was more than that. Gibbie was super strong. He could've crushed Troy's skull. And yet by denying Gibbie his desire, Troy remained the one in control. He shook that idea aside. Holding hot cheerleaders was *Troy's* specialty, he reasoned.

"What are you...?"

Troy ignored him and was already grabbing the blond from under the armpits and balancing him over the toilet.

"Sorry about this, buddy," he said. Grabbing a toothbrush from the countertop, he shoved it to the back of Chad's throat.

At first nothing happened.

Feel it, goddamn it. Troy pushed with his thoughts, his own throat involuntarily constricting, ready to hurl.

The blond's neck and stomach clenched and he writhed to life, clutching the porcelain throne and throwing up unceremoniously. He heaved several more times, filling the toilet with undigested pills.

When the retching stopped, Chad moaned, but the glassy look seemed to be gone from his yellow eyes. Troy lowered him to the bathmat. Several heartbeats passed. One crisis was down, but the question remained: now what?

"We can't just leave him here," Gibbie said.

"I know," Troy replied.

Thirty seconds later, amidst the smell of bile, Gibbie finally got his wish to hold Chad.

"Pick him up," Troy said.

The elder Allstar brother watched in amazement as Gibbie cradled Chad in his spindly arms, as if the muscular cheerleader was as light as a spritz of cologne.

In another half-hour they stood outside the Allstar residence. Gibbie had held Chad close, sprinting the entire time. The little nerd was only slightly winded from the effort. Troy had biked as fast as he could, curious to see what his little brother had in him. He was impressed, and a little disturbed, at how well Gibbie had kept pace. In fact, Troy got the feeling that he was slowing his little brother down.

Troy opened the back door as quietly as he could.

"Damn it, Fred, where are they?" their mom yelled.

"I'm sure they're fine. The police said they sent Troy home."

"How can you be so bloody calm? Our children are *missing!*" she insisted.

Gibbie looked ready to call out, but Troy held his finger to his lips, and then pointed upstairs. They got to the second floor as quietly as they could, and Troy held his bedroom door open.

Gibbie hesitated. "Maybe we should put him in my room."

"Do you really want him waking up surrounded by *Star Trek* mobiles?"

Troy felt the verbal slap as if he were Gibbie himself, just as he'd felt Chad's desperation earlier in the evening.

"Come on," Troy said gently, pulling the blankets back from his bed (they'd been neatly tucked with military precision), and Gibbie set Chad's unconscious form on the mattress.

"He looks so peaceful," Gibbie said.

"He's not," Troy replied before he could catch himself. Occasionally Chad would twitch, and he hoped Gibbie would assume that's what Troy was referring to. But he knew that whatever the blond boy was dreaming, he felt hunted.

"Troy?"

"Yeah, Gibbie?"

"How'd you know he was in danger?"

If this had been a soap opera, soft dramatic music would have risen up and the camera would have closed in on Troy's worried face.

"Later," he said.

Downstairs, Troy was practically suffocated by his parents' arms gripping him tight. He endured it for as long as he could, along with the weepy cries of "my baby, my baby"—and that was just his father—before he finally pushed them both away.

"I'm fine."

That's when their mom noticed Gibbie's shredded shoes. There were blood prints on the tile floor from where the soles of his feet had rubbed raw. It was surreal in their bright yellow kitchen with sunflower trim.

"Oh my God!" She rushed forward.

"This?" Gibbie said, "It's just makeup. Me and the guys are making this video for YouTube. It takes place in the distant future, after zombie cannibals take over the earth."

Their mom sighed.

"Well just clean this up, would you?"

She gave him a hug, and then wrapped Troy in her arms.

"You gave us quite the scare."

"Yes," Troy said, feeling her relief, "I know."

He could also feel the pain in Gibbie's feet.

"Want a lift?" he asked, turning and kneeling.

Gibbie climbed onto his brother piggyback. In Troy's washroom upstairs, Gibbie washed his feet in the shower while Troy brushed his teeth.

"So are you going to tell me?" Gibbie asked, wincing as he picked out a piece of gravel embedded in his big toe.

"Tell you what?"

"How'd you know? About Chad, I mean."

"You wouldn't believe me."

"Troy, I busted through a solid wood door, and carried him all the way back here. I'm super strong." *Some of the time*, he thought. "And look at Chad."

Chad's back was to them, a regular teen from this angle, but turn him over...

"I think something's happened to us," Gibbie whispered, "Maybe it's happened to you too, but different. Did you see him?"

"Well, yeah," Troy replied.

Gibbie's face bunched up with excitement. "With X-ray vision?"

"No, it was not X-ray vision."

Troy stifled his impulse to add the word "dork" to the end of the sentence.

"Déjà vu?" Gibbie pressed.

"Spider sense," Troy countered.

"Really?" Gibbie leaned forward, slopping water onto the floor as he grabbed his brother's muscular forearm.

"Where did the spider bite you?" he asked. Muttering to himself, he added, "And how did you even come into contact with a radioactive arachnid?"

Gibbie looked up into Troy's smirking face.

"You're making fun of me."

Troy pressed his hand against his temple as he felt the rise of hurt anger from his little brother. There was a boiling kettle in Troy's skull, with nowhere for the steam to escape. The pressure just kept building.

"Geezus, Gibbie, could you just stop feeling stuff for five seconds? It's like a marching band in my brain. I'm really starting to get a headache."

Gibbie looked at him incredulously.

"I'm not kidding this time," Troy insisted. "That's how I knew Chad was in danger. I could…feel it. He was scared, and desperate, and I just"— he waved his hands in the air—"I felt him slipping away. Okay?"

"So what am I thinking now?" Gibbie asked him.

"I don't know what you're *thinking*. I know what you're *feeling*."

"Fascinating," Gibbie whispered, and Troy knew his little brother believed him, could *feel* it.

"Clearly something's happened to us," Gibbie went on, "but what was the causal event? What do we three have in common? And are there others?"

He rhymed the questions off like he was pondering what to put in a sandwich.

"Yeah," Troy said, "And how do we make it go away?"

"Make it go away? Are you crazy? We have superpowers! Do you know how many people dream of superpowers?"

"Actually, *you* have a superpower," Troy corrected. "Half the time I feel like yelling, the other like crying. I'm like a chick that's permanently on the rag."

"You saved Chad," Gibbie offered.

"No," Troy corrected, "you did. I banged on his window while he nearly died."

Gibbie looked ready to counter Troy's words but their dad poked his head in through the doorway.

"Okay, guys, I know it's been a long day, but time for lights out." And then he noticed the person in Troy's bed. "Who's that?"

"Oh, uh, well, you see," Gibbie stammered.

"He's my friend," Troy said without hesitation. "Sorry for not introducing you. He had a bit of a panic attack earlier, at the mall, with the whole kablooey thing. He just wanted to lie down. Wasn't really up for meeting new people. I just figured you'd be level if he crashed here."

"Sure, of course," their dad said. "Definitely level."

"Cool," Troy said nonchalantly.

"Cool," his dad echoed in the way older people do in their attempt to bond with the younger folk. "I'll make sure to put out an extra plate at breakfast."

"That'd be great," Troy replied.

"Well, good night!"

Their father clicked off the hallway light and disappeared from view.

Gibbie's eyes narrowed. "Interesting."

"What do you mean?" Troy countered.

"He kind of bought that a little too easily, don't you think?"

"Meaning?"

"Too soon to speculate," Gibbie said coyly.

"Whatever," Troy yawned. "That's it for me for today."

"Really?" Gibbie asked. "I mean, shouldn't we run some tests?"

"Sure thing, professor," Troy said. "Oh wait, I think our CAT scan machine is on the fritz."

"So now what am I feeling?" Gibbie glared.

"Okay," Troy said, "simmer down."

He pulled out his flip pad.

"Run tests on super freaks," he said as he wrote it down.

He showed the pad to Gibbie. "Satisfied?"

"I guess."

The little redhead stepped into the hallway, and then turned back.

"I still think Chad should stay in my…"

Troy closed the door in his face.

"I could break this down, you know!" Gibbie shouted.

"It's your allowance that'll pay to fix it," Troy yelled back. "No comic books for at least a month."

There was silence, and then the sound of stomping footsteps.

Troy stared at the door for a spell, then slowly turned around.

Chad's twitching form was before him. Troy jerked away just a little too quickly. He pulled out a camping mat and unrolled his sleeping bag on the floor. He reached over Chad's head to grab his second pillow. He took a moment to stare at the pretty blond boy, cat eyes hidden behind closed lids, fangs safe within his lips, only his pointed ears left to give him away.

Troy backed away and set the pillow at the head of the sleeping bag. He crouched over it, staring. It looked so…

Safe.

…uninviting.

He looked back at Chad. He'd felt so wild, so free, so…

Hot.

…uninhibited. Everything Troy was not.

He switched the overhead light off, and in the glow of the moon, he did not go to his lonely sleeping mat on the floor. Instead he sat on the bed next to Chad's resting form. The cheerleader's nose wrinkled and he let out a sad little moan.

Troy examined his classmate's body. He gently stroked the smooth forearms and wondered if Chad shaved them. Chad gurgled at the touch, leaning in closer. Troy stroked his hair, his bare back.

"Where did you take me tonight?" Troy whispered.

The wrestler bit his lip, hesitating. He pulled his hand back. He looked once more to his sleeping bag, then to the closed door separating him from the rest of his family. He waited for footsteps, but none came.

He gazed at Chad, and crawled in under the blankets, settling in next to the cheerleader. *Just for a second*, he assured himself. The wrestler put an arm around the blond's muscular body. Troy's heart pounded. With closed eyes and a deep sigh, Troy nuzzled the other boy's shoulder.

It felt so warm and right, so unlike cuddling with Mandy when they'd still been together, Troy constantly trying to follow the recipe he'd seen in movies. Troy's throat constricted painfully, and he swallowed hard. With a force of will Troy pulled away, about to get out of bed...until he realized Chad was staring at him.

Chad's eyes were groggy but open. The wrestler froze. His instinct was to stumble away, to stammer an apology, to explain he just needed a pillow.

But before a word could be said, Chad touched Troy's cheek. They stayed like that, staring at one another, and Troy's mouth grew heavy, a magnet drawn to its opposite charge. Slowly Troy leaned forward, and Chad did not pull away. Their lips met, and Troy's chest swelled with a growing pressure. It filled him, and flowed into Chad and back again. Their kissing grew more fervent, their hands exploring the forbidden territory of each other's bodies. This was wrong, so very wrong, and yet it felt...

Amazing.

And unstoppable.

Their lips parted, and Chad nestled deeply against Troy. The blond no longer felt hunted. He felt found. He felt safe. The sharp teeth, claws, and pointed ears were gone. He looked like himself again. Troy could sense Chad's comfort as he fell back asleep, but what Troy felt was another matter. For just a second it was like they'd been one, and now a huge chasm spread between them. Troy retreated slowly, and crept off into the shower. He scrubbed himself under the hottest water he could stand.

It took him a long time to fall asleep in his sleeping bag on the floor.

Chapter 5

Dear Diary,

What happens when a brother betrays a brother? When someone stabs his best friend in the back? When an outcast and the head cheerleader become bosom buddies? I'll tell you what happens. Drama—with a capital D!

"Devon, my love, I am so sorry for being late!" Lyla Dedarling proclaimed as she bustled through the door of her expansive mansion on her sprawling estate. Under one arm she carried a gleaming black portfolio case. In her other hand was a brown takeout bag with a stapled receipt from Wong's Chinese restaurant. The smell of soya sauce steamed out from the edges.

"There was some terrible thing at the mall tonight," she continued, releasing a huge sigh. "It was an utter nightmare getting out of there."

Devon Dedarling heard his mom, hidden away though he was. Her voice carried. He silently kept typing away on a goth vampire message board.

He flicked the wisps of black locks hanging over his eyes. In the back, his hair was buzzed down to the scalp. His features were delicate, matching a slender build wrapped in skintight black jeans and a Marilyn

Manson shirt.

Lyla Dedarling's heels clicked across the marble floor of the circular foyer and into the kitchen. There was the pop of a cork from a wine bottle, the clatter of a glass, and the gurgle of liquid being poured. The clickity-clack of her heels resumed.

"Dinner's getting cold!"

He let her wander past the indoor pool, movie room, and pilates studio. "Devon?"

The alive are dead. So to be undead is to truly be alive, he typed.

She finally found him under the stairs that led to the sunken garage. His laptop monitor bathed him in a blue light. She twirled her glass of wine.

"There was some terrible thing at the mall tonight..." she began again. Like any performer she knew the show must go on, whether the audience wanted it or not. "But never fear," she said excitedly, "I brought Chinese!"

It was too early for the interesting vampire freaks to be logged on, and Devon's slender stomach rumbled, so he followed his mom into the kitchen. Mrs. Dedarling's squat body busied about, her jacket pushing her ample bosom into a canyon of cleavage. Selling other people's over-priced consumer art to banks, hotels and lawyers' offices took sweat, tears, and, apparently, a hefty rack.

"What a day. The gallery was a beehive, I tell you," she made little *bzzz* noises while pinching repeatedly at the air. "Just when I think it's all about online sales, charge 'em up and ship 'em out I say, bam!" she clapped her hands. "Mega-sale for that new condo going in along the river."

"You mean the one that's going to be little rat cubicles stacked one on top of the other for aging urbanites wanting to reconnect with small-town life while at the same time choking the charm out of it?" Devon inquired.

"Devon," she said coyly, "that sounded suspiciously like an opinion."

"Pass the lo mein," he grunted.

She shrugged perkily, spooning out beef, rice, and sweet and sour pork. "It's going to be sheer elegance, I tell you, *very* boutique. Finally someone's got the vision and the…" she hesitated, searching for the right word. In a fit of daring that told Devon it must have been *quite* the sale indeed, she gave herself permission to say, "…the *balls* to break away from the dreary country chic this town is drowning in. I mean don't get me wrong. I didn't just ride that wave, I practically made Trisha Romance into a household name, and it paid for a good chunk of this." She gestured around the kitchen, at the granite counters, European appliances, and designer taps. "But the past is past!"

She wiped a piece of bamboo shoot from her mouth with a cloth napkin.

"And," she continued, "they aren't falling into that über-sleek non-sense. Even the homosexuals are over that, Allah be praised!"

So that's her god of the week, Devon noted, dipping a chicken ball into bright orange sauce. She filled a glass from a water cooler in the corner. Not once did his mom even pause for breath. "It's all about old nouveau," she prattled on. "The cutting-edge gays—not those Pottery Barn castra-tions—are already leading the way, and as usual, the rest of the world will follow."

She wasn't even looking at Devon as she spoke. She stared off into the air, twirling her water between sips. "Picture a dandy in couture, mixing quotes from Oscar Wilde and Irvine Welsh, then buying an oil portrait in a stainless steel frame from an online auction. That"—she jabbed her bright red fingernail into the air—"that is the future, and the future is now!"

She finished off her glass of water. He loaded his plate with moo goo gai pan, tucked his computer under his arm and got up to leave. Most teens dreaded the inevitable parental question, "How was your day," as if it were an Abu Ghraib interrogation. Devon never had to worry about that query. His mom was still talking about herself, and didn't notice he'd left until he reached the doorway.

"Devon!" she called after him. Normally he'd have ignored her, but from the corner of his eye he noticed she was staring at her glass of water.

He began to smile. He had to force the expression from his lips before turning around to face her.

"Yes, mother?" he inquired with mock innocence.

"Devon Dedarling, did you take the bottled water back to Food Depot and exchange it like I told you?"

He gazed at the chrome Etienne water cooler next to the fridge. Listening to her coo over the bull-necked deliveryman "with the most piercing green eyes" as he installed it had been worse than her going on about the gold earrings she'd just received from a Saudi paramour after a month-long Internet correspondence.

"He has the sexiest mustache," she'd bragged about the sheik, insisting on showing Devon his profile pictures.

Now she stared at her half-empty glass like it was a rattling snake. "Devon..."

"Yeah," he piped up, "I totally exchanged it, just like you said."

To prove his point he marched past her, poured himself a glass of Etienne water from the cooler, drank it in three gulps, refilled his glass, drank that too, refilled again, and drained that also. He went back for a fourth time.

"Okay, Mr. Dramatic, you've proven your point," she conceded. "It's ridiculous you know. I pay for pure spring water, only to be told it's been contaminated at a processing plant."

She drank her glass down, and so did not see her son's crooked smile.

He wasn't exactly sure why he'd lied to her, except that it was more fun than not lying to her. The media said that whatever got into the bottled water was benign. The recall was just a precaution. So it gave Devon great pleasure to know his mom thought she was drinking different water that was safe, instead of the same water that was also safe.

He poured himself another glass, and drank it down.

Chapter 6

That night Devon flipped between various goth message boards while sitting at his desk. Most teens' rooms were rife with self-expression. Not Devon's. There was not a single poster anywhere. His furniture consisted of other people's discards, painted sanitarium-white—a snub to his mother's attempts to Ikea-fy his life.

"Well at least let me get you a Tulpan lamp!" she'd insisted.

The bulb hanging from his ceiling remained defiantly bare. It matched the clean surfaces of his desk, chest of drawers, and even his empty bookshelf. Books, CDs, and school bag were all stuffed into the closet.

"I could have them padded," his mom had offered, gesturing at the white walls with her glass of red wine. "Maybe have a straitjacket in a display case. You know, really invest in the *Clockwork Orange* theme you've got going."

He hit CTRL+TAB on his keyboard, flipping through his message boards. Message boreds were more like it. *Bunch of losers sitting at their computers pretending to be anti-establishment instead of actually doing it,* he raged inwardly.

That included himself, he hated to admit. *If I had the power, I'd turn this town of hicks and wannabes inside out.* The clock on his screen read half past midnight. And so it was that he knew the exact time his life changed.

His free hand tapped idly on the desk. He prayed for inspiration. His fingers stopped tapping. He crooked his slender eyebrows.

His black-painted nails had landed in something gooey. He expected to see it in leftover moo goo gai pan. But the plate was on his other side.

Instead, where his skin touched the desk, it looked as if the white-painted wood had been turned into melted white chocolate. He pulled his fingers away, and stretchy white strands that resembled taffy stuck to the tips. He flicked his wrist and the white bands flew back, squelching onto the desk.

His chair toppled as he took a frightened step back. There was a clatter as his laptop crashed to the ground. He gazed at his right hand, which had been resting on the keyboard. Gooey strands of black plastic reached up from the keys like umbilical cords, one attached to each of his fingers.

From downstairs he could hear his mom snoring as the *Golden Girls* theme song blared from the flat-screen TV in the living room.

He knelt down beside the fallen computer and struggled to catch his breath. He gripped the monitor with his left hand and pulled back with his right. The plastic strands stretched and then gave an elastic snap, landing on the keyboard like spaghetti tossed from a sieve. He tried letting go of the monitor, but now his left hand was stuck, the thumb embedded in the screen.

The computer's built-in speaker made a bleeping noise.

You still there? BloodThirstyVixen995 asked him in a chat window.

He grabbed the monitor with his free hand, and that became stuck too. The more he struggled, the more enmeshed his fingers became. To his horror, the computer began to warp. He bent it into a semicircle, and still the monitor worked. A flashing porn banner featured a pair of buxom redheads making out. Their breasts and winking faces adopted a lurid funhouse-mirror quality as the monitor took on a convex bulge.

He looked towards his bedroom door.

"Mom!" he called. The desperation in his voice made him clamp his mouth shut. He squeezed his eyes closed.

"I don't need her, I don't need her, I don't need her..."

He was panting. His shirt was soaked in sweat. He was starting to tremble. He looked back towards the door as the opening theme of *Mary Tyler Moore* rose from below.

"Mom!" he yelled, no longer caring how scared he sounded. Still no answer.

To hell with her, his mind seethed, and yet he hated that she didn't sense he was in trouble, did not come running, that he was forced to beg for his unhearing mother to save him. He stared at his hands encased in his computer. Tears streamed down his cheeks.

"Please!" he cried one last time.

Chapter 7

Devon Dedarling felt more alone than ever before. His eyes were bloodshot as he stared at his once state-of-the-art laptop. It now looked vaguely like a lava lamp, with the keyboard forming the base. The keys still worked. A bouncing skull-and-crossbones screensaver flickered on the rounded monitor. His clock read 5:33 a.m.

His throat was hoarse from calling for his mom to help—an act of such desperation it left him with the stillness of death inside, and anger, for she was passed out on the couch with her second bottle of wine and her damn old-woman shows, leaving him completely at the mercy of events beyond his control. As the hours ticked by, and his attempts to pull himself free failed, he sat at his desk panting. Slowly, exhaustion took over. His chin lolled forward. Sleep descended upon him. As he dreamed, his fingers slid free.

An hour later his mom came bustling in, without a hint of a hangover, thanks to the can of Energy Xtreme she was drinking. Her cleavage fought against a low-cut red blouse, and her ass was barely contained in a form-fitting skirt.

"It's a brand new day, darling. You don't want to miss the bus," she gushed.

His head snapped up, eyes wide with fright, remembering all too clearly the nightmare of the past few hours.

Get out of my room was what he wanted to shout. Now that she was here the last thing he wanted was for her to see him so helpless. But when he held up his hands, he stared at them in awe and relief. They were free of his computer!

"It was just a dream," he whispered, until he looked at the twisted remains of his computer, and knew the experience had been all too real.

He got to his feet quickly, blocking his laptop from his mom's view. She fussed with a bit of lint on her collar.

"No problem!" he said.

"I know what you're going to say, that you hate being stuck with that rabble of zombies, and quite frankly I don't blame you..." She hid the piece of lint in her pocket and looked up in surprise. "Did you say no problem?"

"Yeah," he said eagerly, "I'll be down in a second."

Her eyes narrowed. She shifted left a bit, and Devon mirrored her.

"What are you hiding?" she demanded, her heels clicking forward.

"Nothing!" he insisted.

"I will not have you frying your brain with drugs. That's what college is for," she said, briskly pushing him aside.

Her lashes stood on end and her eyelids opened so wide it was a wonder her thick layer of rose-colored eye shadow didn't crack.

"What have you done!" she gasped.

She was pointing at the computer. Her brightly painted fingernail shook. He waited for her to shriek at him, and shriek she did.

"It's brilliant! Allah be praised! My son *is* an artist! I knew it!"

Her hands were pumping the air as if she were a cheerleader.

"Oh Devon." She hugged him tightly. "I still remember you coming home from kindergarten with your finger paintings and I'd ask you what they were, and you'd say an elephant, and I'd say it was the best elephant I'd ever seen and you'd tear it up in a rage and say in the most sullen voice, 'It doesn't look anything like an elephant' and you'd slam the door in a huff. An artist's temperament, I told that no-good father of yours!"

Tears bubbled in her eyes and she wiped them with a lace hanky stenciled with the letter D.

"I am going to stop blubbering, I am going to stop blubbering," she chanted, and a moment later she did, suddenly all business again. "Let's get a proper look at this masterpiece."

She turned on his white desk lamp, angling it at the computer.

"Bold," she said. "I can honestly say I've never seen anything like it."

For a second Devon thought it would get him out of school today, but when he suggested it, her response was "You're an artist, not a deadbeat," before shoving his bag into his arms and pushing him out the door.

Less than an hour later, Devon sat in homeroom class, surrounded by rabble. Everyone else was blathering on about the mall exploding—or being hit by an earthquake, depending on which news report you believed. But the real news, that six members of the Nuffim High student body had been forever changed, did not make a single supper-hour show, newspaper headline, or Facebook profile.

What's happening to me? Devon wondered as he sat at his desk, or, as he liked to call it, a cubicle to prepare him to become an office drone—like that was ever going to happen. But right now all that was forgotten. For most of the night his hands had been stuck in his computer. They must have slipped free when he fell asleep. For just a moment he worried this was a result of too much masturbation.

"...Leonardo was not just an artist, he was also an inventor." His teacher, Mrs. Cordial, began the day's art lesson. "He designed wings, in the hopes of letting man fly. But one of his greatest obsessions was the human anatomy."

She put up a transparency of a naked man superimposed on himself, making him appear to have four arms and four legs, encased in a circle and a square.

"I'm sure most of you recognize this. The Vitruvian Man. In this drawing, a study of human geometry, Leonardo combines art and science."

"Science," Devon whispered, quickly pulling out his chemistry textbook. He flipped to a page with a diagram of a water molecule, next to a hydrogen atom.

"Most matter is actually empty space," it read.

He gazed at the images of charged particles and how they interacted with each other to create the semblance of solidity. He recalled how it had felt having his hands inside his computer, like there were tiny magnetic hooks on his palms. He felt hot and cold at the same time. His fingers began to sink into the textbook, and he pulled them out quickly before anyone could notice.

I have to learn how to control this, he thought, whatever "this" was. The normal thing would be to go to a hospital, but he'd be damned if he gave his mom the satisfaction. Nor was he the only one in the senior class plagued by the need to master a new power.

"You look rough," Markham said to Mandy.

"You try doing your hair and makeup when you can't see yourself," she snapped, snubbing his look of confusion. She was too focused on trying to catch Chad's attention. He was wearing an Aberbombie shirt, which was weird, because he *hated* Aberbombie. Too conventional, he claimed. But more importantly, he'd ignored Mandy's panicked calls after the mall blew up last night, and now he was too busy casting glances at Troy to notice her.

Troy sat as straight-backed as ever, but from the corner of his eye, he too seemed to be looking at Chad. And then there was Liza.

Out of habit, Markham rolled up a piece of paper, putting it in his mouth, gobbing it with spit, and then shoving it into the hollow outer shell of his disposable pen. He raised it to his mouth. There was barely need to aim with Liza's mass of tangled black hair. Mandy put a restraining hand over his.

"I wouldn't do that if I were you," she said.

"Whatever," the pretty-boy jock scoffed, firing the spitball.

It hit Liza's cheek. Mandy waited for the tall girl's scream to level the classroom, but all she did was briskly write something in her notebook.

Hit List. Homeroom.

"I can't take this anymore," Mandy muttered to herself, and she grabbed Chad's hand. He blinked, finally noticing her.

"We need to talk," she whispered to him.

Five minutes later they met in the girls' washroom.

"Mandy," Chad said, casting nervous glances in the mirror, making sure his eyes and ears looked normal, "I really can't talk about your crush du jour, 'cause things are really messed up right now."

"You think?" she demanded.

She opened her purse and pulled out her lipstick. As soon as she brought the red tip close to her mouth, her lips began to grow fuzzy. She pulled the lipstick away, and her face returned to normal. Chad blinked repeatedly.

"Did you just...?"

"It gets better," she said.

She repeated the process, except with mascara. Her eyes disappeared, and he stared into an empty cavity in her skull. She pulled the applicator away, and her missing eye fizzled back into view. She handed him the mascara bottle.

"Throw it at me."

He hesitated.

"Come on, faggot, throw it at me."

He tossed it and the bottle bounced off a crackling shield in front of her. The field faded away and she began to cry.

"Chad, I don't know what to do."

He walked over and picked up the fallen bottle. He wiped the tears from her eyes and hugged her tight.

"It's going to be okay."

"How can you say that?" she said, "I'm a freak."

"Yes, you are. And so am I."

He unscrewed the cap on her mascara and pulled out the curled tip.

Gently, he began applying it to her lashes. They remained visible when he did it.

"Chad, no offense, but your whole gay thing, it's not the same," she argued. "We don't exactly have an invisible freak girls' pride parade, okay?"

"Mandy, for the first time since I can remember, I'm not even thinking about being gay," he responded.

He told her everything that had happened the night before. About his eyes, the claws, the pills. Somehow he failed to mention how her ex-boyfriend crawled into bed and made out with him.

It was nothing, he assured himself.

"It's so *Valley of the Dolls*," she said, referring to his overdose, "If you're lying..."

"I'm not."

"Show me," she said, arms folded over her small breasts.

"I..." he hesitated.

"What?"

"I'm scared."

"You're not sure if you can turn it off," Mandy concluded.

He nodded.

"I get it," Mandy sighed, staring in the mirror. "We're freaks. Now what?"

Before Chad could answer, the door flew open. Mrs. Cordial stood there.

"I just got a call from the principal's office," she glared. "Chad, the school counselor would like to see you."

"Crap," Chad whispered softly, looking to Mandy for rescue.

"I think you're on your own for this one," she said.

"*Now*," the teacher emphasized. "And you might want to grab your bag from class. I think this will take a while."

Chapter 8

Chad sat with his knapsack on his lap in the school counselor's office. The counselor slammed a pair of jeans down onto his desk. The denim was shredded in places. The gouges were long and wide.

"The police found these next to the highway. Your wallet and cellphone were nearby."

Chad reached for his pants but the counselor, a mountain of a man with a receding hairline, pulled them back.

"I can explain," the teen said.

The man's stern face stared at him.

"Dad…," Chad began.

"I am not your father in this office."

"Okay, coach," Chad mocked.

"Right now I'm not the football coach either. I'm the school counselor. Got it?"

"Aren't counselors supposed to be impartial?" Chad countered.

"Don't you impartial me, mister. When I got home the front door was smashed in, you were nowhere to be found, there were pills everywhere, the police discovered your clothes near a…"

"Cruising park?" Chad offered.

"I was worried sick!" his dad yelled.

Despite himself, Chad was touched.

"I've watched you run loose ever since your mother died. I figured it was just a phase. That you'd grow out of…" he twirled his wrist in a mincing manner.

"Out of what?" Chad asked. "Being a queen?"

His dad ignored the question.

"I thought I could keep my mouth shut until you graduated high school, but this is too much." He picked up the pants and waved them in Chad's face. "Do you have any idea how humiliating this would be for me if anyone found out?"

"Aren't we supposed to be discussing *my* feelings?"

"You shut your mouth before I smack it!"

Chad silently looked about the cramped office, at the polished trophies atop the filing cabinet, at his father's teaching certificate in a dusty frame, anywhere but at his father's cleft jaw and thick neck.

"This is going to stop, right here, right now," he declared. "You're grounded."

"You can't ground me," Chad replied. "You're not my dad in this room, you're my school counselor."

His father kicked a beaten-up steel garbage can against the wall. Cans of Energy Xtreme went flying out of it.

"Do you even know what your life would be like here without me?" he demanded. "Huh? Do you?"

"Because it's so great right now?" Chad replied.

His dad snorted.

"I'd like to see how cocky you'd be if your dad wasn't the coach of the football team. You'd have the daylights kicked out of you every other day."

"Gee, thanks, Counselor Lenwick."

His father skirted around the desk and grabbed Chad by the front of his shirt, yanking him out of his chair.

"My guys look up to me, so they keep their hands off of you."

"Not all of them."

His dad flinched.

"What's that supposed to mean?"

"It means your all-star from last year didn't just play for your team, and you weren't his only coach."

His dad pushed him back into his chair. Chad grabbed his pants, stuffed them into his bag, and sprang towards the door.

"You sit your ass down!" his dad ordered.

Chad gave him the finger and slammed the door behind him.

In the school hallway, Chad walked up to the nearest locker and punched it as hard as he could. He was surprised by the impressive dent he'd made. He unclenched his fist and looked at the sharp talons growing from his fingertips.

Calm down, he told himself, *find your center.*

His breathing slowed and his claws retracted.

"Chad!"

His nostrils flared and he didn't have to turn around to know who it was.

"Hey, Gibbie," he replied.

"I'm glad I caught you. Open your backpack."

"Open my...?"

Already Gibbie was pulling it from over Chad's shoulder.

"Listen," Chad said, "I really appreciate you and your brother helping me out last night, and your parents giving me a ride in to school with you, but..."

Gibbie unzipped the backpack, pushed aside the shredded jeans without even blinking, and declared triumphantly, "I knew it!"

Gibbie pulled out an empty bottle of Etienne water.

"This has to be it."

"Has to be what?" Chad asked.

"I'll explain everything at lunch. Meet me and Troy in the audiovisual room."

"Uh...I'm not really the audiovisual club type, if you know what I mean."

Chad made the shape of an L with his right thumb and pointing finger and placed it over his forehead.

Gibbie knew exactly what he meant, but he had no time for it.

"You're changed, Chad. The eyes, the ears, the claws."

"*Shhht,*" Chad hissed, looking around to see if anyone had heard.

"I'm changed too," Gibbie said excitedly, "and so is Troy."

"You guys...are like me?"

"Yes! Well, no. Not exactly like you. But we're different now. I'm super strong. Some of the time. I carried you all the way back to our place!"

"You carried me?" Chad scoffed.

Gibbie grabbed Chad by his muscular arms and lifted him to prove his point. Well, Gibbie *tried* to lift him. His on-again, off-again super strength was most definitely off.

"Listen, you seem like a nice kid," Chad said. "But I'm a little busy hating my father right now, drowning in a crisis, and I have to get to my next class."

Gibbie trailed after him.

"Don't you remember anything from last night?"

Chad recalled plenty—the forest, the pills, Gibbie's dreamy older brother holding him tight.

"Wait...," Gibbie begged.

He jumped ahead of Chad and held the hall door shut. Chad grabbed the handle and tried to force it open. It remained firm under Gibbie's palm. Gibbie didn't notice. His shoulders sagged.

"Fine," he sighed. He gripped the handle to open the door for Chad and with a frustrated yank he ripped the door right off its hinges. It hung in the air, easily held up by Gibbie's twiggy little arm. Chad stared.

The front door was smashed in, Chad's father had said.

Chad gave Gibbie a wide berth while walking through the portal.

"I'll see you in the audiovisual room at lunch."

Chapter 9

Gibbie sat alone amidst transparency projectors, slide machines, VCRs, and DVD players. He stared at the clock above the door. His eyes then wandered down to the cue cards on the desk in front of him.

"Dear friends," he began to read, "since before the dawn of Marvel Comics, man has dreamed of..."

The doorknob turned and Gibbie stood excitedly when he saw Chad. Then Mandy came in after him.

"What's she doing here?" Gibbie demanded.

"She's changed too," Chad replied.

"Yeah," she echoed, her voice all Valley-girl ferocious, fist planted on her cocked hip. "I'm totally changed too."

"You seem the same to me," Gibbie said sourly.

"Where's Troy?" Chad asked, his voice cracking.

"Here," the wrestler said, careful not to brush against Chad while entering the room. They eyed each other like a pair of stray dogs. "Let's get on with this. I have to get to the weight room."

Gibbie stared at them all in disbelief.

"Guys, we can do stuff, and you're all acting like pumping iron and being catty are still the most important things in the world."

That was Gibbie's interpretation, and based on surfaces, he was right.

But Troy knew better. He could feel the roiling panic beneath Chad and Mandy's thin veneer of bitchiness. They were both ready to crack, and were distracting themselves the only way they knew how—by making light of the situation. As for Troy, he just dissociated.

"Well not *the* most important," Mandy said defensively, her voice on edge. She was gazing into her compact and trying to reapply her lipstick. "This is hopeless," she muttered, shoving the mirror back in her purse.

"I didn't see you skipping your morning episode of *Star Trek* today," Troy said to his little brother.

"That was research!" Gibbie shrilled.

"Hey," Chad piped up, "our physics teacher said that faster-than-light technology could never actually happen."

Gibbie sputtered, "That is highly contentious!"

"All right, boys," Mandy said, clapping her hands. "We're sorry, Gibbie. Social retards are people too. Please continue."

"What exactly is your ability, Mandy?" Troy asked. "Super bitch?"

Chad chortled and quickly covered his mouth under Mandy's glare.

"I can turn invisible," she said to her ex, "*And* I can make a force field."

"Really?" Gibbie asked, but to Mandy's surprise, he wasn't looking at her. His thick glasses were focused on Troy. After a few seconds the jock nodded.

"She's telling the truth."

"Am I to assume you're Lie Detector Man?" Mandy sneered. "Great power, *very* scary."

"Actually, I'm an empath," Troy replied. "So suck it."

"Never heard of it," she shrugged.

"Just give me a second!" Gibbie interrupted, waving for them all to pipe down. With his other hand he clicked on his laptop, which was hooked up to a projector. So began Gibbie's PowerPoint presentation.

"Dear friends," he began to read. "Since before the dawn of Marvel Comics, man has dreamed of having superpowers."

A cover image of *The Avengers*, issue No. 1, looked back at them, with classic comic book characters like The Hulk and Ant-Man.

"Be it from mutation, genetic engineering, or freak accident," Gibbie continued, "Many are the ways superpowers can be gained."

Chad kept staring at the cleft of Troy's chest, revealed in his workout tank top. Troy felt the gaze, bringing a flush to his own cheeks. He pulled his jacket shut. Chad's head snapped back to the presentation, allowing Troy to gaze at the smooth skin of Chad's neck without the blond noticing. The cheerleader hid behind a campy persona; Troy found strength in his own robotic control. Both facades now seemed brittle around the other.

This is trouble, Troy thought, remembering how good it felt to hold his classmate. Troy knew he wanted to do it again, a desire he must not give in to. If he did, who knew what emotions might come pouring out. He needed containment to neutralize this threat. He then noticed Mandy, and he hated the idea he got, but he hated his desire for Chad even more. Troy looked down at his notepad, and wrote, "Get back together with Mandy."

Gibbie clicked his computer and an image of a bottle of Etienne water materialized on the screen. Next to it was an article with the headline: "Etienne Bottled Water Recalled."

"This article appeared yesterday," Gibbie said, "after some sort of non-toxic contamination got into the Etienne bottled water plant in Calebraton. But not every bottle was successfully recalled. Troy and Chad both drank Etienne water yesterday. I had it force-fed to me."

He looked to Mandy. "Crap," was all she said.

"So what was the contamination?" Troy asked.

"Officially," Gibbie said, changing the image to a blown-up portion of the article, "they're saying fluoride."

"Doesn't fluoride just make your teeth stronger?" Troy pressed.

"It does," Gibbie agreed, "and many municipalities add it to their water supply for that reason. But some research indicates it can have unexpected effects on the brains of kids. *And,* I don't believe this was just any kind of fluoride."

The image changed, and a drawing of a chemical structure was before them.

"I found this in *The Journal of Radiological Research.* Its fluoride, but it's attached to a mild radioactive isotope, the kind injected into people during certain medical procedures."

"So?" Mandy asked.

"So..." Gibbie pressed the mouse again and a graph appeared. "Etienne's stocks went up five years ago after it was announced that their research team had a breakthrough in fluorination that would specifically target teeth."

"You think some of this experimental fluoride got into their regular supply accidentally?" Chad asked.

"And I don't think it targets enamel," Gibbie replied. "It concentrates in the brain. That's why it never got past the lab stage."

"So because somebody wanted to make stronger molars, now I can turn invisible?" Mandy asked skeptically.

"Well," Gibbie responded, "I'm sure there are other factors. I mean, maybe it's only teens that are affected. Our brains are at a specific developmental stage. Maybe that's what makes us candidates."

"So then there could be a cure," Chad said.

"Sign me up," Mandy said.

"Amen," Troy agreed.

"You guys are kidding, right?" Gibbie said.

"No," they said in unison.

"Look," Gibbie said, clicking on the computer's mouse. "This is Deanna Troi, from *Star Trek.* She's an empath, like our Troy."

"Wait a second," Mandy said. "All she can do is say, 'Captain,

I sense I have big boobs.' *That's* your power?"

They all looked at her in surprise.

"It's not geeky to watch *The Next Generation*," she said defensively.

"He may also be able to control other people's emotions," Gibbie said.

"I can?" Troy asked. "I mean, yeah."

"I said maybe," Gibbie clarified, "but that's just it—there's so much we don't know about this. Shouldn't we, I don't know, try out what we can do first before looking for a cure? I mean, think about the possibilities..."

"Listen in on other people's gossip," Mandy mused.

"Psych out the competition," Troy added.

"Sniff down potential husbands," Chad concluded.

Gibbie sighed. "I was thinking make the world a better place."

"Oh," said Troy, Chad and Mandy, looking abashed. "Of course...right...yeah."

Mandy put her hand up.

"Hey, is there one of your dork superheroes with a crazy powerful scream?"

"Uhm...yeah...a couple. They're not the most popular characters, so I don't think I have any on my laptop, but I'm sure I could download some images."

Troy gave Gibbie the "you're a retard" look, then turned to Mandy.

"What's got you so scared?"

"FYI and PS, I'm not scared," she sneered.

Troy pointed both his thumbs at himself. "Empath." He pointed two fingers at her. "Scared."

"Well, you'd be scared too if you'd been right in front of Liza when she took out the mall, by yelling," Mandy snapped defensively.

"So Liza's one of us too," Gibbie said.

"If she's a supervillain, does that mean we get to go kick her ass?" Mandy asked excitedly.

"Mandy," Chad interjected, "maybe it was an accident. None of us knew what we could do, and it's not like we can really control it even now."

She slouched in her chair.

"Fine."

"It's kind of weird, don't you think?" Troy said. They all looked at him. "I mean, Liza barely even talks, and now she's got this killer voice? And Gibbie, no offense, but you're not exactly The Hulk. Now you're stronger than Schwarzenegger on radioactive 'roids."

"And Mandy," Gibbie continued, "the girl who likes to be seen..."

"...and touched," Chad added.

"...can now turn invisible and has a force field," Gibbie concluded.

"And then there's Chad," Mandy snapped, "the guy who shaves his ass..."

"...and balls," Chad chimed in.

"Is wolf boy," Mandy concluded.

"I feel more like a cat, actually," Chad purred. "So what about Troy?"

"You mean the guy with the emotional range of a rock?" Mandy asked. "Now he senses other people's feelings."

"Maybe the isotope latches onto some sort of repressed part of the brain," Gibbie speculated.

The bell rang and they all looked to Gibbie.

"Now what?" Mandy asked.

"I...uh...," he stammered.

He hadn't thought much past his PowerPoint presentation.

"We meet again," Troy interjected. "Tonight."

"Right!" Gibbie nodded. "After school!"

"After wrestling and cheerleading practice," Troy corrected.

"Some of us have lives," Mandy pointed out.

"And somebody needs to talk with Liza," Troy added.

"I'll do it," Mandy offered.

Troy looked at her suspiciously, but he felt nothing malicious coming from her. In fact, there was a tinge of guilt.

"Okay," he said.

It was not the best decision he would ever make.

"So," Troy said to Mandy as he picked up his bag, "do you need a ride later tonight?"

"Well," she replied, "as the super bitch of the group, I wouldn't want to put you out. Besides, unlike some people, I actually have a car. But thanks for offering to pick me up in your mom's minivan. Very fetch."

Don't let her raz you, Troy told himself. *That's why you snapped earlier.*

"I guess I had that coming," he conceded.

She looked surprised by that, but sloughed it off.

"Whatever," she replied, and then said to Chad, "I've got to go to the ladies' room."

"No prob, I'll wait," Chad replied.

She pushed her way past Troy.

He was about to follow her out when Chad grabbed him by the arm.

"What're you doing?" Chad demanded.

"Going to the weight room," Troy replied, his expression frustratingly neutral.

"That's not what I mean."

"I don't know what you're—"

"Mandy," Chad cut in. "She dumped you and now you're offering her a ride?"

"So?"

"So, you're not getting back together with her."

"That's not really your business."

"It became my business last night," Chad said meaningfully. For just a moment, Troy felt the rush of desire wash off the shorter boy, and it was reciprocated, just like when they'd been in bed together. But on the surface...

"You leave Mandy alone," Chad said, holding up a claw menacingly. "Got it?"

"Chill," Troy capitulated. Chad was only two breaths away. It would be so easy to stroke his chest, to lean in close, to press their lips together. Troy took a sudden step back, holding his hands up in peace. "I got it."

Chapter 10

Devon Dedarling walked with unusual briskness down the halls of Nuffim High, careful not to touch anything. His hands had already accidentally trashed his textbook, a pencil, and the water fountain. The janitor stared at the mutilated porcelain in confusion. But despite the mishaps, Devon was slowly losing his fear of his fingers getting permanently caught in something. Already it was getting easier to slip his hands in and out of things. And every time, his excitement grew.

Nor did he dwell much on how this had happened. He knew it had to be the contaminated water he'd drunk. He'd read enough comic books before his parents divorced—back when he still had interests—to realize superpowers developed from freakish environmental exposures.

He also knew the next step was always to figure out the extent of his abilities; but first, he had to pee. He stopped in front of the boys' restroom, but did not go in. Something about the girls' washroom door had caught his attention. It was shaking, he realized. A screw popped loose from the handle and rattled across the floor, stopping against the soles of his black Dockers.

He pushed the door open a crack, and caught sight of Lezzie

Liza serenading herself in the girls' washroom. She leaned on a radiator, eyes closed. A look of bliss filled her face as she sang "I'm Not a Girl, Not Yet a Woman." The entire room vibrated like a tuning fork. He stepped inside, closing the door behind him.

The song eased downwards, as did the room's reverberations. Liza opened her eyes and, as soon as she saw him, clamped her mouth shut. All lay still.

"Your voice," he said, "it's different, isn't it?"

Liza bit her lip and slowly nodded.

I'm not alone. The realization made the inside of Devon's chest swell with relief. Normally he'd berate himself for such a weakness, but the truth was, he'd been denying how freaky all this really was. He'd long thought of Liza as something of a kindred spirit. Like himself, she was not willing to walk the high-school walk, nor talk the in-crowd talk.

He held up his hands and smiled.

"I'm different too."

In the driveway of the Allstar residence, Mandy slammed the door of her car. Chad got out the other side. Troy stood on the porch. Baskets of flowers were hanging all around him.

"Where's Liza?" he asked.

"I looked for her, I couldn't find her. I'm sorry," Mandy said. "She must have ducked out of school early."

"It's okay, babe," Chad said, rubbing her shoulders. "We'll find her on Monday. What could happen in one weekend?"

"You have got to see what I did to my computer last night!" Devon told Liza excitedly, opening the door to his bedroom.

He stopped within the white walls, staring at his white desk.

"What's wrong?" she asked.

"It's gone," he said, rushing forward.

He heard the front door opening.

"Mom?!" he shouted.

Her heels clippity-clapped up the stairs.

"Darling, Mommy's home early!" she chimed, stopping in his doorway. "And look, you've brought a little friend!"

"Where is it?" Devon demanded.

"Where's what?" his mom replied with a look that was far too vacant to be genuine. "Oh, your art piece! Devon, my love, I have the most wonderful news! I sold it!"

"You *what?*"

"To one of my best overseas clients. I couldn't resist sending a JPEG, just to brag about my son the artist," she gushed. "And Mr. Ganoush Ganosh—Ed to me, of course—well, he absolutely *had* to have it. I suppose I should've asked..." She said it in a tone that implied how ridiculous *that* would have been. "My darling"—she pinched his cheek—"he paid a mint!"

"Get it back," he seethed.

"Impossible!" she chuckled. "FedEx is good, but they're not *that* good. Oh, Devon, I know this is hard for a young artist, but you mustn't grow too attached to your work."

"You goddamn pimp!" Devon screamed.

"Language, young man. We have a guest." She blushed, looking at Liza apologetically. "And I am *not* whoring out my son's talent. I've waived my usual agent's fee, and you, my little Michelangelo, now have a very handsome sum in a joint bank account. And as a little bonus to get you started on your next project..." She pulled out her wallet and began counting out five hundred dollars.

He stared at the bills she placed in his hand. And then he lost it.

"I don't want your stupid money. I want my computer back!"

He pushed the cash towards her, intending only to shove it away from himself, yet he did so much more. His hands and the bills landed on her exposed cleavage, and sank within.

He yanked his arm back in surprise. The bills stayed stuck to his mom, melded with her breast, as if she, like his computer, were clay under his touch.

"What have you done?" she gaped in horror, trying to pull them off, to no avail. Veins ran into and out of them. She ripped part of a bill in half. Blood slowly trickled from the torn ends.

She screamed. It was a howl Devon had never thought he'd hear coming from this perpetually chattering woman. It terrified him even more than when his fingers had been stuck in his laptop. Somehow he'd always seen his mother as both invulnerable and unflappable.

He reached towards her, trying to help, even if he didn't quite know how.

"Get away from me!" she shouted, smacking his hand and backing away.

"Mom, listen," he said.

"Your computer," she said. "*This* is how you did it?"

She pulled out a handkerchief, dabbing at the bleeding bill in her breast.

"I have to get to a hospital," she sobbed.

"Wait!" Devon begged.

He grabbed at her jacket and she shoved him back onto his bed. He lay there, panting. Her eyes were wide with fear now. She turned and ran.

"I'll drive you there!" he shouted, clomping down the stairs in her wake.

"I'm not getting into a car with you!" she shouted back.

He knocked his way past her and blocked the door. Her hand-kerchief was now soaked with blood. She picked up the phone in the hallway and dialed 9-1-1. He jumped forward and grabbed the body of the phone. It turned into a mush of plastic, seeping through the sides of his fingers. She yanked the phone cord from the wall and quickly wound it around his wrists, all the while eyeing his fingers like they were ten bobbing cobras. He pulled himself away from her, his shoulder slamming into the wall, his feet slipping on the carpet. He fell sideways and smashed his head against a cabinet, dropping to the ground.

He blinked to clear his hazy vision. His mom remained a blur of red.

"I'll be back," she vowed yanking the door open, "with the police."

"I can...," he mumbled in a daze, "I can fix this."

"I believed in you," she said, "and I was wrong."

She turned to go. The setting sun blazed behind her through the open door. Her shadow caressed her fallen child. A looming figure stepped behind her.

"Liza?" Devon gurgled, his eyes narrowing to bring her into focus.

Mrs. Dedarling turned rapidly. Her heel snapped. She teetered, her ankle wavering as it tried to stabilize her bulk. Liza raised a black skillet.

Mrs. Dedarling dropped her purse, trying to shield herself with an arm.

"Help!" she shouted.

Her voice fell on the deaf trees of her huge estate. The skillet smashed into the side of her face. Devon watched his mother fall next to him. Her pearl earring smacked and cracked against the marble floor. He shook as he struggled to his feet. Liza's meaty grip helped him up and held him close. Devon wasn't used to being touched, but he was too shaky to pull away.

They both looked down at his mom's unconscious body. A huge bruise was forming on the side of her face. The hundred-dollar bills were still merged with her skin. The bleeding had stopped, clotting over the torn paper.

"I...I didn't know what else to do," Liza said, her voice trembling.

"Now what?"

Devon heard Liza, but underneath he also replayed his mother's words: *I believed in you, and I was wrong.* The echo sent numbness down his spine.

"Now," he said, gazing back at his mother, "now we make art."

Chapter 11

Devon and Liza stared at Mrs. Dedarling's solid wood dining room table. Mrs. Dedarling seemed to lie peacefully atop the antique import that stretched from one end of the room to the other. A chandelier was ablaze with light. All around her were place settings—her very best china and glassware.

"Sing," Devon whispered.

Liza obeyed, her voice a tinge harsh, yet beautiful all the same.

The table vibrated. The silverware rattled in a convulsive dance. A wine glass cracked. Mrs. Dedarling's eyes popped open. She tried to move, but her entire back was now a part of the table, as was the side of her face, hiding the growing bruise where Liza had smashed her with the skillet.

Devon's face loomed in front of his mom's one visible eye.

"What have you done to me?" she demanded. The words came out slurred; a quarter of her mouth was melded with the table.

He peered at her through a jeweler's loupe, the kind used to appraise precious stones. He gazed closely at the points where her body and the table became one. There were blue veins in the wood, and lines of tree grain in her skin.

His tone was flat as he spoke.

"I wonder how much your overseas clients would pay for this piece."

Troy, Gibbie, Mandy, and Chad gathered on the floor of Gibbie's room. Mandy looked around at his collection of *Battlestar Galactica* posters.

"It's exactly as I imagined," she said.

Chad lay on Gibbie's bed reading *Cosmo*, and Troy was pretty sure his little brother was about to pee himself with excitement. Troy didn't dare look at the hunky cheerleader.

Mandy was idly going through Gibbie's bookshelf.

"Not a *Gossip Girl* fan, I see." And yet her snide tone died down as she pulled out *Star Trek: The Next Generation Technical Manual.*

"Do *not* bend the corners," Gibbie warned.

"The Enterprise has force fields, doesn't it?" Mandy asked.

Gibbie nodded. "And the Romulans have cloaking technology."

"What?" she said as Chad gave her an amused look. "Geek can be chic."

Troy handed Gibbie a back issue of *Muscle Men: The Magazine for Serious Pumpers*, and told him, "Check out the article on weightlifting and the central nervous system." Gibbie gave the book *Cats for Dummies* to Chad, and Chad handed his *Cosmo* to Troy.

"How to Drive Your Man Wild in Bed." Troy read the title of the article Chad had been reading.

"You might learn something," Mandy teased.

Troy blushed. So did Mandy. So did Chad. Gibbie made a mental note to skim the article when no one else was around.

"Flip ahead," Chad said. "There's a quiz on emotional intelligence. Maybe that will help with your whole empathy thing."

And so they began to figure out what they could do. An hour later, Gibbie lay on his brother's bench press in the basement. The bar above him was stacked with weights. Gibbie grunted, trying to push it up. It wouldn't move.

Chad and Mandy sat on the basement stairs.

"You know, he is pretty hot," Mandy said.

"Gibbie?" Chad sputtered.

"Please." She was appraising Troy.

The older Allstar brother wore a sleeveless shirt and shorts that showed off his quads and calves.

"I thought you were over him," Chad replied, a worried furrow on his brow.

"Totally," she said with a grossed-out look on her face.

Chad recognized this as stage one of a Mandy crush.

"Still," Mandy mused, "it is kind of sweet the way he's trying to help his brother, and he's all take charge and stuff."

Step two.

"Uh-huh," Chad agreed unenthusiastically. "And stuff."

"You have to concentrate," Troy ordered his little brother.

"I *am* concentrating," Gibbie whined, twisting his body this way and that, as if he just needed to adjust his angle to get the weight up.

"Not the way you need to," Troy insisted. "You're all in your head. I can feel it. You have to move outside your brain, and into your body. Remember what that article said? Visualize your consciousness in your chest, and squeeze. Stop flexing your temples and start flexing your muscles. Engage your whole nervous system, not just your brain. Come on, man. You can do this."

Gibbie gripped the bar once more, pushing hard.

"Chest, shoulders, triceps," Troy chanted, "chest, shoulders, triceps..."

Gibbie let go a fearsome grunt, and the bar lifted upward. He began pressing it easily, cranking out twenty reps without even breaking a sweat.

"Now that's what I'm talking about!" Troy shouted.

Chad and Mandy found that their powers were activated differently from Gibbie's. Chad made his claws grow. Under his command they receded. He made his eyes turn cat-like, then baby blue.

"I can turn them on or off on their own, or..." He focused and his ears grew pointed, fangs sprouted from his gums, and his claws returned all at the same time. "It's almost like flexing a muscle in my brain *and* focusing myself in whatever part of my body I want to go wild. And to turn them off, it's like relaxing a muscle. Mandy, try it."

They watched as she winked in and out of view.

"Oh my God!" She clapped, jumping up and down excitedly. "Save the cheerleader, save the world!"

"That is the gayest thing I have ever heard," Chad replied.

Hand on her hip, Mandy gave him her fiercest 'oh no you did not' look.

He held his palms up in peace.

"I'm totally turning it into a cheer. *Now.*"

"I want to run a couple of tests," Gibbie interjected, rolling up the sleeves of the white lab coat he wore overtop of his Cobra Commander shirt.

Half-an-hour later, back in Gibbie's room, Mandy stood in the center of a series of circles, each one larger than the next.

The first consisted of miniature starships resembling the Enterprise. The next circle was made from plastic green soldiers. The next, Lego men. The one after that, He-Man figurines. Each ring was about half-a-foot away from the next.

"All right," Gibbie said, "turn invisible."

Mandy winked out of view.

"See if you can expand your invisibility field."

The row of spaceships dissolved from sight.

"Notice how the floor stays completely visible," Gibbie said. "Her field's moving outward, not downward. Keep going."

The plastic soldiers vanished.

"Any more?" Gibbie asked.

They heard a little grunt from her, and the Lego characters began to fizzle, and then popped back into full view.

"One-and-a-half feet seems to be your upper limit," Gibbie said, writing it down on his clipboard pad.

Mandy blipped back into sight, and wiped the sweat from her forehead.

"Let's try out your force field now," Gibbie instructed. "Let's see what you can knock over."

She concentrated and the field buzzed around her.

"See if you can knock down the first circle," Gibbie instructed.

She tried to push the field out, but nothing happened.

Gibbie moved one ship right next to the crackling shield.

"Try some more."

She grunted, squeezing her eyes shut.

The little ship grudgingly fell over. She gasped and the field dropped.

"It would seem that you *can* expand the field, though only marginally. You might want to work on that."

"I might want to take some Aspirin," she replied. "I don't know about you guys, but I feel this all in my head."

"Fascinating," Gibbie said. "Any luck turning invisible and turning on your force field at the same time?"

She shook her head.

He scribbled once more on his clipboard. "Perhaps they use the same part of the brain, or parts that balance each other out, like antagonistic muscles." He looked to Troy to see if his brother had caught the fitness reference. The others looked at Troy as well.

"What?" he asked.

"Three down," Gibbie answered. "Only you to go."

But testing an empath's abilities was not quite so easy. Gibbie's power seemed to work by moving his focus into his body. Mandy was all in her head. Chad appeared to be a bit of both. Troy's just seemed to be on all the time.

"Did the *Cosmo* quiz help?" Chad asked.

"Apparently I'm a passive-aggressive taker/withholder," Troy replied.

"Shocking," Mandy added.

Troy gave her the finger.

"So what am I feeling now?" Mandy asked.

"Annoyed," Troy replied. "Oh wait, that's me."

Actually, he was getting something from Mandy—affection, and attraction.

"I...you..." he stammered, unprepared for the interest he could sense from her, the polar opposite of earlier today. Chad watched with growing worry.

"So, Troy, any luck turning your power off?" the blond said a little too loudly, giving Mandy a warning look.

"Um, kind of," Troy said. "If I shove all the emotions into a room in my head, lock the door, I can mostly ignore the pounding as they try to get out."

"Can you separate them?" Gibbie asked. "Can you tell which are my feelings and which are Chad's feelings?"

The jock looked at the muscley blond and, unusually for Troy, he grew red.

"Still working on that," he lied, scratching the back of his neck and avoiding eye contact with anybody.

"Right." Gibbie jotted down the details, "And you said that you can sometimes recognize a person without seeing them, like their feelings give off a fingerprint."

"Or a reflection," Troy added.

"I have an idea," Gibbie said, putting down the clipboard. From his desk drawer he pulled out a contraption that looked like a bulky PalmPilot. He began moving it in the air in front of his brother.

"Interesting," Gibbie said.

"What is that thing anyway?" Troy asked.

"Medical tricorder," the younger Allstar replied. "If these readings are correct..."

"Give me that." Troy grabbed it from Gibbie's hands and held it up. "This is a *Star Trek* toy."

"No it isn't," Gibbie protested.

"It says Mattel on it."

"I...I have to go to the washroom," Gibbie said, rushing out.

Troy popped a panel open on the back and yelled after him.

"It doesn't even have batteries in it!"

Chad and Mandy laughed, oblivious to the true tests lying ahead.

Chapter 12

Monday morning arrived.

Troy got up at six o'clock and jogged to school, as usual. The jock picked up his pace when he felt someone approaching from behind—and easily catch up.

He looked at Gibbie, running at his side, wearing one of his new Aberbombie and Stitch T-shirts. It had a print of a regal-looking Indian chief, and the words underneath, "Native Aberbombian."

"Wow," Gibbie said, not even panting, "so this is why you get up so early. The world's so quiet and peaceful."

"It *was*," Troy corrected. His brother didn't notice.

"So I was thinking, maybe I'll try out for the track and field team," Gibbie said.

"I didn't know you were into that sort of thing," Troy replied.

"Well," Gibbie said, easily keeping pace while Troy began to feel a tightening in his calf, "now that I'm super strong, I should do something with that. Originally I was thinking football—"

Troy sputtered.

"—but it would be way too easy to hurt someone. Track, on the other hand... I could run, throw stuff, jump. I won't always come in first—too suspicious. But you know, we're changed now.

Our lives should change too, right?"

"I hadn't really thought about it," Troy lied, panting a little as he tried to keep pace with Gibbie. "It's not like my power's really going to change my life."

"Well," Gibbie said, "instead of becoming an engineer like you were going to, maybe you should be a counselor."

Troy struggled to process this possibility.

"Anyway, do you mind if I run ahead?" Gibbie asked. He didn't wait for an answer before picking up his pace, zooming off into the distance.

Troy came to a stop and stared at the trail of dust raised in his scrawny brother's wake.

"Hey Liza!"

Liza's Amazonian frame started, and she slammed her locker door shut. Mandy stood in the hall where Liza could have sworn she'd been alone.

"I didn't see you there," Liza said.

"Yeah, I know," Mandy said smugly, "I'm super sneaky that way."

Liza nodded in that slow way of hers.

"I remember."

"Of course you do!" Mandy chirped as if she were a Disney animated songbird. "Which reminds me. We really should talk about what happened at the mall."

"I don't remember any of that," Liza lied.

"Come on," Mandy said, taking Liza by the shoulder. The larger girl looked at Mandy's arm like it was a black widow. "Let's go somewhere more private."

Devon watched from a few lockers down. Liza made a cringing face, but there was no help to be found.

"Listen, I know the whole blowing-up-the-mall thing wasn't

your fault," Mandy said as they stood out by the school dumpster.

"You do?" Liza regarded her hesitantly.

"I know that you would never hurt anyone on purpose."

Liza flashed back to hitting Devon's mom on the head with a frying pan, and what they did to her after. "*I wonder how much your overseas clients would pay for this piece,*" she heard Devon say.

She shook it off and realized Mandy was looking at her expectantly.

"Sorry," Liza said, "I missed that last bit."

"Silly!" Mandy giggled. "I was saying that you're not alone. You're not the only one who can do something special."

Liza's eyes widened in alarm.

Devon.

"There's you"—Mandy pointed at her—"there's me, and Chad, and Gibbie, and Troy."

"They can all..."

"Do stuff," Mandy said perkily. "You kind of have to see it to believe it. Well, except for Troy. Not really the glitziest of powers, to be honest. And you have to show them what you can do! Just not at the mall, okay?"

Liza nodded dumbly, looking about for some sort of escape.

"And don't worry, we've all been practicing and getting better at what we can do. We can totally help you with that whole destructo voice thing. So what do you think?" Mandy said cheerily, slapping her hands together and hunching her shoulders excitedly. "Want to hang?"

"So what did she say?" Chad asked Mandy as they filled their trays in the cafeteria.

"She said she'd think about it," Mandy replied.

"Hold the light mayo right there, lady!" Chad said, stopping the lunch line. "Am I to understand that you, the most popular girl in school, gave Lezzie Liza the social invitation of the century and she has to *think* about it?"

"I don't know what's going on in this crazy upside-down world of ours," Mandy agreed as they sat next to Troy. He was picking at his chili.

"Why so glum, chum?" Chad asked.

"Nothing," Troy lied, his gaze turning towards a sudden uproar on the other side of the cafeteria.

A blonde cheerleader was hoisted into the air atop her chair. She squealed in delight. Whoever was doing the lifting was hidden by the crowd of onlookers.

"Gibbie?" Mandy asked.

"Gibbie," Troy replied. "He showed up at the track team's practice this morning. Guess who their newest member is."

"I thought sports tryouts ended ages ago," Chad said.

"Apparently they were very impressed with his discus throw," Troy replied. "I think it landed in China."

"China?" Mandy tittered, putting a flirtatious hand on Troy's forearm. "That's practically my homeland."

Chad looked at her askance.

"Uh, your parents are Korean," the blond cheerleader said, giving Troy a warning look. Troy pulled away from Mandy's touch.

"Well, I said *practically*," she snorted defensively.

"Is showing off like that such a good idea?" Chad asked, jerking his head towards Gibbie's display of strength.

"And what happened to making the world a better place?" Mandy added.

"I think he's starting to figure out it's fun being strong and fast," Troy observed sourly. "I'll go talk with him."

But instead of making a beeline for Gibbie, Troy felt his attention pulled elsewhere. He was being watched. It made his skin prickle, as if fingers were running along the down on his forearms.

He knew that feeling. His eyes flicked over to a table full of raucous jocks, and there sat Jesse, Troy's former best friend.

Their eyes met for the briefest of moments, before Jesse's gaze darted back to his book, Stephen King's *The Drawing of the Three*. A couple of the other guys held up scores as if they were Olympic judges, rating girls as they walked by.

"I'll catch you guys later," Troy said, stepping away from the table and looking at Jesse's smooth skin, strong cheekbones, and shaved scalp. Gibbie's words during their jog that morning rang in Troy's head.

We're changed now. Our lives should change too, right?

Another cheer rang up for Gibbie Allstar, Mr. Popularity.

Gibbie was surrounded by other students and appeared to be arm-wrestling a strapping quarterback. His little brother was pretending to struggle.

He's playing, Troy knew.

"Ha-tchoo-loser," someone sneezed as Troy just stood there.

It was Markham. Two seats down, Jesse gave Troy a "you're on your own" shrug. Troy could feel Markham's satisfaction as his teammates smacked him encouragingly. Troy stepped over to their table, leaned in and whispered in Markham's ear.

"Hey tough guy. How'd it feel having my little brother toss you across the mall? Want him to do it again? Right here, right now?"

He felt strong as he said it, a hammer smashing into glass, and Markham suddenly looked fragile. Troy felt the other boy's feelings churn, his innards shrinking like Saran Wrap thrown into a campfire.

Maybe Gibbie was right, Troy mused.

Maybe I can control people's emotions.

All it took was the right words, the promise of a little social humiliation, a mental push, and voila.

He felt Jesse watching. He met the handsome youth's eyes.

The Stephen King book remained in his hands, but was otherwise forgotten.

"What do you think, Jesse," Troy asked. "Am I a loser?"

His former best friend said nothing—didn't need to, in fact. Troy could feel what Jesse felt—sadness, loneliness, need buried deep away. *He wants his friend back.* The wrestler looked over at where Gibbie was surrounded by a hive of people. And then there was Chad and Mandy leaving the cafeteria together. Everybody had somebody. Troy had his wrestling teammates, but what he really needed was his bud, especially with so much screwed-up stuff going on.

"How's wrestling?" Jesse asked.

Troy pondered that, staring at his friend.

"Not as much fun as football was," Troy said.

Jesse's expression shifted, radiating hope and excitement. He was so different from Troy, bold without being overbearing, while Troy was a stone.

"The team's not the same without you," Jesse said.

Words, just words, but conveying perhaps a deeper meaning.

I'm not the same without you.

"I know tryouts are over, but..." Troy hesitated. "But maybe, I don't know, maybe you could make an exception?"

"Seriously, man?" Jesse asked, his face genuinely brightening. The warmth in his chest was like a balm to Troy.

"If that's cool with the team's captain."

Jesse grinned. "I'll have a word with him."

Gibbie let his knuckles get dangerously close to the table. The bulky quarterback he arm-wrestled was Riley, who seemed determined for a rematch. He put all his weight onto his hefty arm to force Gibbie's down. The smaller boy kept waiting for this to feel hard, but it wasn't. The cheerleader he'd hoisted in the air earlier turned away. "I just can't look!" she cried.

Without even a grunt, Gibbie slammed Riley's hand onto the table.

"No way!" guys shouted. "That has got to be fake!"

Gibbie held up his arms.

"Nothing up my sleeves, ladies and gentlemen. For my next act..."

Troy caught the closing moments, and now slunk forward, putting his hand on his younger brother's shoulder.

"Could I steal you for a minute?"

"In a second," Gibbie said dismissively.

"Now would be good."

Troy said it in a tone that barely rose above his normal flatline, and yet a hush descended on those in earshot. He'd been thinking about the time when Gibbie used to beg him to bring him trick-or-treating with the big kids, would have done anything to tag along, promised him all his candy, whatever he wanted.

"Sure," Gibbie said, his voice trembling softly.

Troy led him to the pop machine and then rounded on him.

"What are you doing?"

"I'm just having a little fun."

"Gibbie, we need to keep a lid on this, okay? All those heroes in your comic books, they have secret identities, right? It's for a reason. What do you think would happen to us if the world knew what we could do?"

Gibbie shrugged.

"Don't sulk," Troy said. "Just use that brain of yours, okay?"

"I am using my brain," he replied, "And I know what you're doing."

"What do you mean?"

"I've gone from feeling like I'm on top of the world to feeling like a piece of garbage. I'm not manic, Troy. You're doing this to me."

"No I'm not," Troy protested. "I just want you to remember who you are."

"I remember who I am, Troy, and I hate him, okay?" Gibbie said, pushing past his brother. "But I guess he's all you'll ever let me be."

A pair of tall-stem glasses clinked together in the home of what was left of Mrs. Dedarling. School was done for the day. Now the real learning began.

"To new projects," Devon said. He and Liza stood in the dining room. His mom's corpse remained merged with the table. Flies buzzed around her sinking flesh.

Liza's hand trembled and she spilled a bit of her champagne.

Devon steadied her hand.

"Easy there, my angel," he said.

His angel. Her heart fluttered at that and a smile twitched at the corner of her lips. She took the jeweler's loupe from Devon. It was easier looking at Mrs. Dedarling through the eyepiece, as if she were a thing and not a person. Devon stroked Liza's hair. She'd given up on anyone ever doing that since her grandfather died, yet here she was.

I deserve some happiness too, she assured herself.

"So guess what happened to me at school today," Liza said as she peered at Mrs. Dedarling's nails disappearing into the table's surface. "Mandy asked me to hang out with her."

"So that's what that was about," Devon grunted.

"Isn't that hilarious?"

He looked doubtful.

"She's setting you up for something."

"Maybe," Liza agreed, "but there's something I need to tell you, and I'm sorry I didn't tell you before. It's just—"

"It's okay," he said, "trust takes time. Tell me now."

"Mandy can turn invisible."

"She can what?"

"It's not just you and me who can do stuff," Liza said.

"Is there anyone else?"

She bit her lip. "Chad, Troy, and his brother Gibbie."

Devon nodded slowly. "Did you tell her what I can do?"

"Of course not," Liza said, "I don't share your business."

"Good girl," he said. "Let's keep it that way."

"You should have seen her face when I told her I'd think about it, like I was turning down dinner with Justin Timberlake or something."

"I think you should accept," Devon said, pouring more champagne.

"Yeah right," she snorted, but looking at his face, she said, "You can't be serious."

"Have you ever seen the movie *Mean Girls*?" he asked.

She nodded, her clunky mind starting to pick up speed.

"You want me to infiltrate them."

He grinned wickedly.

"It will be our masterpiece."

He kissed her on the mouth, with just a bit of tongue, and then whispered in her ear, "I'm so glad we met."

"Me too," Liza blushed, and then with surprise asked, "You've seen *Mean Girls*?"

He shrugged. "I'm a big Tina Fey fan. She does a wicked Sarah Palin."

Chapter 13

Troy felt an unexpected halo of joy around himself as football practice wrapped up for the evening.

"Good to have you back," Coach Lenwick said.

"It's good to be back," Troy replied. He was surprised by how much he meant it. Wrestling was cool, and he was team captain, but it was very individualistic. Football meant you really had to play like a team. It meant you belonged.

"Hold back, Allstar," Jesse said to him as everyone else headed for the locker room. "There are a couple of plays we need to go over if you're going to be ready for tomorrow's game."

"I really didn't think I'd be on the field that soon."

Jesse shrugged. "Come on, man, it's all about forward motion."

The plays they went over weren't anything special. Troy was hesitant to even call them new, but he was not about to complain. By the time they got to the locker room, the last of the players were filing out. Chad was the only person remaining. His short shorts and pompons were packed in the bag over his back. He wore a button-down, short-sleeved shirt that hugged his biceps tightly. He was dressed not unlike the way Troy often did.

"Hey Troy, I thought I'd wait in case you needed a ride home."

Chad held up his keys.

"No, I'm cool," Troy said.

The male cheerleader looked from Troy to Jesse.

"Oh."

Troy could feel Chad's whiff of jealousy.

"Chad..."

"Whatever," Chad said in an off-hand manner. He walked out, trying to look nonchalant.

Jesse made a low whistling sound as the door closed and they both stripped off their football gear, down to their pants.

"Looks like someone's got a crush on you."

Troy winced. "Quiet. He'll hear."

"A dog wouldn't have heard that," Jesse defended himself.

Troy sighed.

"A cat might have."

"Come on, man, forget the cheerleader. You and me, we're back, the dream team reunited. Ain't nothing can stop us now."

"Yeah," Troy said, a little nervously.

"Easy, man," Jesse said, "I know things got a little weird, but that was just one time, just two friends horsing around. No big deal, right?"

"Sure," Troy said. Still, he couldn't resist the occasional sideways glance at his friend's powerful thighs in his tight football pants. A silver eagle was hanging from a chain, nestled in the cleft of Jesse's big chest.

Troy reached out and held the pendant.

"You still have this," he smiled wistfully.

"Of course," Jesse replied. "Don't you still have yours?"

"Somewhere," Troy replied.

"Well dig it out," Jesse ordered, smacking his friend's butt.

Troy felt the wave of heat in Jesse's temples. It could just be that the radiators were turned up too high or...

"Come here," Jesse said, wrapping his bulging arms around his friend's slightly smaller but no less muscled form. Against his better judgment, Troy hugged back, hard, his forehead pressing into the crook of Jesse's neck.

"I really missed you, buddy," Jesse said.

"I...I missed you too," Troy replied. His grip on Jesse tightened for a moment, and then they stepped away from each other, their hands lingering on each other's smooth skin for just a moment too long.

Jesse cupped Troy's jaw, and they stared into one another's eyes.

"We said things wouldn't get weird this time, remember?" Troy said.

"Yeah, man, I remember," Jesse replied, but still he did not take his hand from his friend's face. Troy could pull away, but it felt good, and right. He tried to push the feeling away, but having Chad walk out in a huff, coupled with the waves of warmth washing off Jesse, coupled with Troy's own...

Loneliness.

...attraction—it was like gongs in his head. He was exhausted from practice, and pushing down the encroaching emotions was like gripping sand.

"Jesus, dude, stop twisting yourself into a knot," Jesse said. He guided his friend and they sat on a bench, leaning against the lockers.

"Seriously, man, it is great having you back," Jesse said, squeezing Troy's leg.

Troy lolled his head back, eyes closed, enjoying the sense of being touched.

Jesse started massaging the hard muscles. The hand started moving upward. Troy grabbed his friend's wrist.

"We can't do this again."

Troy stared into Jesse's eyes and the resistance wavered.

"You have really pretty lips," Troy said, feeling as if he were very far away.

"Prettier than Chad's?" Jesse countered, flashing that big smile of his.

"What?" Troy snorted with a laugh that almost sounded stoned. For an empath, Jesse's feelings were intoxicating, especially since they matched Troy's own.

"I saw the way you looked at him," Jesse answered.

"Well..." Troy hesitated, before nodding slowly. "Since you ask, Chad's lips are prettier. Sorry, bud, he's got you beat in that department."

"Ouch!" Jesse said, playing along. "That's cool, that's cool, the boy's got fine lips, I'll give him that."

"And a great ass," Troy said with uncharacteristic abandon. Only Jesse brought out this side in him. Only with Jesse did Troy feel funny and flirty and free.

"Are you telling me you tapped that?" Jesse challenged.

"Touch me here," Troy said, ignoring the question and placing Jesse's hand on his chest.

"You like that?" Jesse teased.

"Meh," Troy shrugged, "Chad does it better."

He started laughing at that.

"That's two," Jesse warned, his grin growing even wider. "But that's cool. I'm glad you fooled around with Chad. Means you're finally figuring it out."

Troy reached over and began rubbing the stubble on the back of Jesse's scalp.

"Figured what out?"

"You tap your boy toy, and call it a day."

Troy dropped his hand to rest on Jesse's boulder shoulder.

"It wasn't like that. It was..."

"Special? Right. 'Cause you two are in love."

"I never said *that*. But I don't know...there's more to him than meets the eye."

"Man, what you've done is so genius, I'm starting to think even you don't get it," Jesse said.

Troy stared at him blankly.

"See, you pick a guy that you are never going to fall for, 'cause, let's be honest, Chad? Hot, hot, hot, and nelly, nelly, nelly. Ain't no way you're ever going to develop feelings for him. It's cool. You get busy with the little fella, and then have your girlfriend to hang on your arm at parties, get married, whatever."

"Chad's not nelly," Troy said defensively. "I mean, he is..."

Troy felt like he was betraying Chad. Jesse didn't notice. He began kissing Troy's fingers.

"The down low is the way to go," Jesse said. "Guys like us, we're so straight even the straight guys want to do us. That's the way to keep it."

"On the down low," Troy repeated, trying to wrap his mind around the idea.

"That's right, my man. Forget friends of Dorothy. This is the millennium. It's all about the DL. My mom told me all about it."

"Your mom?" Troy said.

"Yeah, man, she saw it on *Oprah*."

And then Jesse was done talking, and deftly pulled Troy's unresisting lips to his own.

Chad's face was a twisting storm. He stood outside the change room door. His ears were pointed. He heard every word. Could hear what they were doing now. The blond glared at the basketball court.

"I am *not* going to be treated this way," he vowed, remembering how Jake had left him for a football scholarship. Now Troy and Jesse...

With a deep breath, Chad turned, prepared to go on his way, letting Troy go on his. And then Mandy emerged from the girls' locker room.

"So I've been thinking," she said, rummaging in her purse, "my approach with Troy has been all wrong—you know, going from totally aloof to completely needy. I need to find the right balance so I don't scare him off the way I did Jesse."

"Mandy," Chad interrupted, getting a very vindictive idea.

"Yeah?" she looked into her friend's very serious face.

He jerked his thumb over his shoulder at the boys' locker room. "There's something you need to see."

Troy knew he was being reckless. Fooling around with Jesse, in the boys' locker room, no less. That went beyond mental. If they were caught... Already he could feel their social standing crumbling beneath their feet. But bigger than that was the feel of Jesse's lips, and their bond from many years of friendship, deepening with every kiss.

I can be on the down low, Troy assured himself. *What's one more secret?*

It all seemed so doable. This felt like heaven after all, until "Hung Up," by Madonna, began to play. Jesse pulled his lips from Troy's chest.

"Who's there?!" Jesse yelled.

There was no answer. Troy blinked in confusion.

"Was that your cellphone?" Jesse demanded.

"No," Troy said.

"Well it wasn't mine." Jesse began throwing open lockers, searching for a spy. "I am going to kill whoever is in here!"

"Maybe somebody just forgot their phone," Troy offered. But he knew that wasn't the case. Someone was here. He could feel her.

There was a clatter of heels on tile, echoing clearly, and there was a splash in a pool of water as if someone had stepped in it, but there was no one to be seen. The door opened of its own accord, and then slowly closed shut.

Troy clenched his fists.

Mandy.

Troy grabbed Jesse's arm.

"Do *not* touch me!" Jesse yelled, pushing his friend away. "Are you crazy? If word of this gets out, I will kill you!"

"But," Troy said, "what about what you said earlier? About us being the guys even straight guys want to do?"

"How high are you?" Jesse demanded. "Nobody's going to look up to a couple of faggots. That's why it's called the down low, 'cause that's where it stays."

Jesse glared at Troy like he was the biggest retard ever.

Jesse quickly rammed his legs into jeans, yanked a T-shirt over his head, and jerked his bag off the bench. When he slammed his locker shut, the sound was like a gunshot ringing in Troy's ears.

"We should talk," Troy said.

Jesse rounded on him. "Not a word. Do you hear me? This did *not* happen."

Troy's head hung low as he buttoned up his shirt, not daring to look at Jesse as his friend stomped out.

Chapter 14

When the tones of "Hung Up" began playing from the phone in her hand, Mandy failed to realize the sound was coming from her— she was too mesmerized by the sight of Jesse macking with Troy to register something so banal as a novelty ring tone.

It was not until Jesse yelled "Who's there?" that she snapped out of it.

And then she ran, her heels clicking audibly on the concrete floor.

Bursting out of the gymnasium, she grabbed Chad, enveloping him in invisibility and pushing him towards the exit. Outside by the dumpster, they popped back into view. Chad's stomach tightened.

"What did you see?"

"Exactly what you wanted me to see, asshole!"

She punched him hard on the shoulder.

"You knew," she shouted. "You know you knew, and you didn't tell me!"

"I...I...," Chad stammered.

"You goddamn piece of twinkie trash!" she shouted.

She kept hitting him, punch after punch, on his back and his arms, even a couple of swift slaps to the side of his head. She pushed him into the dumpster and grabbed his shirt tight in her grip. Buttons popped off it.

"How long, Chad? Huh? How long have you been keeping this from me?"

His breathing was ragged. He stared into her serious face.

"I...," he hesitated.

"Tell me!"

"Not long."

She pushed him hard onto asphalt. He didn't even try to fight back.

"Since the night at the mall," he said. "Troy, he took me home, and he got into bed with me and we...I... I'm so sorry, Mandy."

She towered over him. He looked ready to speak. She spat in his face. He cowered and did not wipe her saliva away.

"I'm sor—" he tried to apologize.

"Don't." She held up a warning finger. "I *never* want to speak to you again."

He reached for her and her force field sprang into place.

"Go hang with your fag friends and have a good laugh at stupid Mandy," she said. "I'm not your goddamn hag!"

She marched off towards the parking lot.

When she reached her yellow VW Bug, Liza was leaning on the hood, waiting.

"What are you...?" Mandy asked, totally confused and wiping away tears.

"You said we could hang out sometime," Liza explained. "Are you okay?"

"In what parallel universe do I look okay?" Mandy snapped, then, taking a deep breath, said, "Sorry. It's just...kind of bad timing."

"Mandy."

She turned. It was Troy, his hair disheveled, shirt untucked, fingers clenched into fists.

"Who the hell do you think you are?" he shouted, and it was like hammers battering her insides.

"I..." Her mouth gaped.

"What the hell were you thinking?" he demanded. "Do you have any idea what you've done?"

"Lied to you?" Mandy shouted back. "Humiliated you? Made you look like a fool? Well, let the punishment fit the crime."

He blushed.

"That isn't fair, I never meant..."

"Well neither did I."

Liza just kept staring at the ground. She coughed awkwardly, and the other two remembered that she was there.

"Hey," he said to Liza, "we're not normally like this."

"It's cool," she replied.

To Mandy he said, "Your cellphone. Please tell me you didn't take any..."

He didn't even have to finish the sentence. The wave of guilt from the cheerleader said it all.

"I'll erase it," she said.

And he knew she spoke true.

He just never bothered to ask Liza what she would do.

The two girls watched Troy walk back to the gym, ignoring Chad.

"Sorry about that," Mandy said to Liza. "How about I give you a ride home, and we'll hang out tomorrow, I promise. Okay?"

"Sure," Liza said.

They drove in silence, Liza occasionally eyeing Mandy's cellphone.

"Turn right here," Liza said. "Now left...oh, slow down, this is it."

Mandy took in Liza's home—the weeds, the mailbox tilted at an angle, the peeling paint on the sagging front porch. Liza waited for the cheerleader's usual scathing remarks, but all Mandy said was "Sorry again about today."

"It's okay. You seemed pretty upset. You know, I might be able to help."

"I don't think so," Mandy replied tartly.

"No, really, I've been practicing, just like you guys, but with my voice. It's good for more than just blowing stuff up. I'll show you."

Gently, Liza began to sing.

Mandy tilted her head, considering this unexpected song, delivered with such grace from a form that was anything but graceful.

"That's really pretty," Mandy said, her words coming out slightly slurred.

Liza kept singing. Mandy's eyelids began to flutter.

"What are you...," she said drowsily.

She never finished the sentence, her chin lolling to her chest.

Twenty minutes later Liza and Devon gazed at Mandy's yellow VW.

"You sure you want to let her go?" Liza asked. She looked at Mandy the way she'd looked at Mrs. Dedarling through the eyepiece—as if she were a thing. It was fair enough, Liza figured, considering how the cheerleader had looked at her all these years.

"Yeah," Devon said, "I still need to hone my craft. Besides, won't it be fun when her little video gets out?"

"Which reminds me," Liza said, holding up Mandy's cellphone, "I should put this back in her purse."

When Mandy's head jerked up with a start, she blinked rapidly and looked around the inside of her car in a daze.

"Wow, you were really out," Liza said next to her. "I guess I don't know my own strength."

"Yeah," Mandy agreed, wiping the saliva from the corner of her mouth.

"Well, thanks for the lift!" Liza said cheerfully. "See you at school tomorrow."

"Sure," Mandy replied, the car door slamming shut behind Liza. The cheerleader looked down at her purse. Her cellphone poked out. She looked at Liza suspiciously, and then shook her head. Liza was the gentlest soul she knew.

Mandy took the phone, went through her video log and found the one of Troy and Jesse. She watched it for a few moments. It ran like a cheap porn loop, doing nothing to capture the bliss she'd seen.

She pressed delete.

When Mandy pulled into her own driveway half-an-hour later, she rammed the brakes, jerked her keys out, and slammed the door behind her.

"What are you doing here?" Mandy demanded, glaring at Chad.

"Begging for forgiveness," he said. "I screwed up, I know I did..."

He chased after her as she tried to get past him by going around back. She turned invisible. His nostrils caught her scent. His ears twitched, locking onto the sound of her steps. He sprang left and she walked right into him.

"That's cheating!" she cried, fizzling back into view.

"Please." He hugged her tight. "You're my best friend. I need you. Everything keeps changing so fast, and I'm scared. I...I betrayed you. I'm sorry, okay? I did a bad thing, but I don't want to be a bad person, and I don't want to be a bad friend. I should've told you about Troy. I just didn't know how."

She looked at him finally. He still held her tight. It felt kind of good, truth be told. Even in this short time, she had to admit she'd missed him.

"You're not a bad person," she grumbled, "but you *definitely* messed up."

"I did, I know I did," he agreed, stepping back.

"Chad, I can handle Troy being gay. I can handle Jesse being gay. I can handle you messing around with Troy. It explains a lot, actually. But to send me into the locker room like that..."

"Was it hot?" he asked.

"Oh my God, yeah," she confessed. "I thought I was going to wet myself."

"Please tell me you took a video."

She pushed him away with a light touch.

"I deleted it."

"You *what?*"

"Chad, I don't want to be a bad person either."

He nodded grudgingly. "You still should have showed it to me first. Friends?"

"Yeah," she said, "friends. But the next time you and Troy make out, I get to watch. Deal?"

"Mandy!"

"Well," she shrugged, "it's not like you actually like him, right?"

Chad said nothing.

"Oh my God, you do!"

"No!" Chad protested. "After Jake, I swore to myself no more closet cases."

"Chad and Troy, sitting in a tree..." Mandy cried as she opened the door of the house and pushed Chad inside, still chanting, "K-I-S-S-I-N-G!"

Troy sat at his desk in his bedroom. He wrote and wrote and wrote. It was a flurry that wouldn't stop until he clenched his pen so tight his fingers seized up. He leaned his forehead on his fists, trying to quell the shaking tears coming from his body. With a deep breath he pushed them away.

He set down his writing pad and lay his fingers on his keyboard.

He googled the word "gay."

Chad and Mandy sat in her living room eating butter-free popcorn and watching *Sex and the City* episodes on DVD.

"It's kind of weird," Mandy said.

"I know," Chad agreed, eyes focused on the TV screen. "Carrie and Aidan? I mean, what did she ever see in him?"

"No, dumbass. Troy being a homo. He's gay, you're gay, Gibbie's gay."

"Do you really think Gibbie's gay?" Chad asked.

"Uh...he pops a load every time you come into the room."

"No he doesn't. Does he?"

Mandy nodded knowingly.

"Wow," Chad said, "a gay geek."

"It seems a bit too much to be a coincidence," Mandy went on, "that all the guys who got powers are gay."

"Well," Chad said, "Gibbie was saying that probably only younger brains would be affected by drinking the contaminated water *and* that there might be other limiting parameters."

"Since when do you use words like 'limiting parameters?' God, you're starting to talk like him."

"I know," he bragged, "I'm super smart now. But anyway, maybe it only affects gay brains. Jake once said that our brains are different. Maybe it only works on queers. I mean, look at Liza. She's pretty much the biggest dyke I've ever seen."

"Literally," Mandy agreed.

And then a horrified expression slowly overcame her.

"Oh my God," Mandy said, gripping her chest.

"What's wrong, pumpkin?" Chad asked.

"If the only people who get superpowers are the gays, then I'm... a dyke?"

Chad turned the TV off and angled his body to face his best friend.

"*That* is crazy talk. There is no way you're a lesbo."

"Are you sure?" Mandy asked.

"Come on! Gay men and lesbians hate each other, and we're super best friends. And look at you, girl. You look fantastic. Not a whisker in sight!"

"That's true," she laughed a little nervously. "I mean, I don't look like k.d. lang, right?"

"Love her old stuff, though," Chad said.

" 'Constant Craving' is in my all-time top twenty," Mandy confessed.

They stopped, worried by that.

"I'll delete it from my iPod!" she promised.

Chad pulled back slowly.

"It may not be enough."

"What do you mean?" Mandy demanded.

"Well, I've been thinking. You're a total babe, right?"

"Right."

"So not exactly the diesel dyke poster child. But then again, look at the chicks on *The L-Word*. I mean those WeHo bitches are *fierce*."

Mandy looked ready to protest, but nothing would come out of her mouth.

"And," Chad continued, "it's not like you actually like straight guys. Let me ask you this: Do you like pussy?"

"Well, I like *my* pussy."

A pained expression came over his face.

"Oh hell," she cursed, "I'm into snatch."

Chapter 15

Dear Diary,

You should totally have seen what went down in homeroom today.
One word, two syllables: AWK-WARD!

The next morning, Troy was one of the first students to get to homeroom. He waited by the door as his classmates piled in. When Jesse arrived, Troy tried going up to him, but the taller youth brushed right by without even glancing at his once best friend. Troy didn't know where to look after that. He went to his desk and pulled out his flip pad. He crossed "Talk with Jesse" off his list.

At the desk next to Troy sat Chad. Chad looked at something he'd written in his own notebook. It was a heart with the words "Troy and Chad forever." He quickly slapped the binder shut, but he realized Troy wasn't even looking his way. Chad's shoulders sagged, and reopening his binder, he began drawing thick edges around the heart.

The biggest stir arose when Mandy arrived.

Chad's pencil fell from his nerveless fingers, his doodling forgotten.

"Jesus Britney Christ," he swore.

Mandy's long black hair had been shaved down to the scalp. Her jeans were baggy and ripped; a chain ran from her belt into the wallet stuffed into her front pocket. She wore a white tank top, and now had a nose ring.

She stopped at Troy's desk and leaned in close.

"Sorry about yesterday, brother. My bad." she grabbed him by the shoulder and squeezed it hard. "Never be ashamed of who you are. Solidarity," she said, tossing a pink triangle pin onto his desk.

He clutched it quickly and stuffed it away.

Mandy took her usual seat behind Liza, who gawked at her. Mandy ran her hands through Liza's thick locks.

"I love it how you're so butch, and yet so femme at the same time. Good for you womyn—that's womyn with a Y," she said to the class, holding up a finger in warning.

As Mrs. Cordial began taking attendance, Mandy leaned forward and murmured into Liza's ear.

"So I was thinking, maybe we could hang out tonight and rent *The Incredibly True Adventure of Two Girls in Love*. What do you say?"

"I...uh..."

Liza's phone buzzed on vibrate mode. She flicked it open and read the text message that had just been sent to her.

It read, "Do it."

She looked up and saw Devon, one seat over, looking at her meaningfully.

"Okay, sure," Liza said, bobbing her head from side to side in an attempt to mimic Mandy's usual ditzy enthusiasm.

Mandy blew a gum bubble, let it pop, and then sucked it back in. "Killer."

After school that day, Liza found herself surrounded by hues of pink and baby blue, accented by frilly white curtains. She sat with

Mandy on Mandy's bed. There was a stack of *Vogue* magazines on the floor. Liza picked one up. The cover of supermodel Gisele had been defaced with the word *oppressor*.

Liza set the magazine down.

"*And so I reclaim this cut*," Mandy read.

"*My wound, my bleeding slit.*

"*For it is no sheath, no vestibule for some man's sword,*

"*Vagina, you ask?*

"*Trojan-ina, I say.*

"*For this hole is me,*

"*And it will fill you,*

"*Until you bleed.*"

Mandy closed the book *Dyke-otomies*.

"Lesbian poetry's pretty cool, huh?"

"Amazing," Liza yawned. "This has been..."

"The best night ever?" Mandy asked.

"Sure," Liza said, putting on her sweater.

"You're going?" Mandy asked.

"Yeah, thanks for the tofu and couscous salad."

"But..."

"I still have homework to do," Liza said. "You stay there. I'll show myself out."

The door clicked behind her.

Mandy held up another book and yelled in her wake. "We haven't even gotten to *The Joy of Lesbian Sex!*"

"It was awful," Liza said as she brushed shellac onto Mrs. Dedarling's corpse. "Lesbians should be banned from writing poetry. Remind me again why I'm hanging out with Mandy."

"To gain her trust," Devon replied, carefully painting his mother's nails with bright silver polish.

The doorbell rang. Liza started.

"Don't worry," Devon replied, "I ordered takeout."

Liza opened the front door and stared at a broad-shouldered man in his early 20s. He could have done with a shave, but his blue-collar buffed body made up for it. He wore a jean jacket overtop a white T-shirt. It was very James Dean.

"Uh, hi," he said to Liza, "are you SexBombTripleX?"

"I...no...I..." she looked back at Devon. He nodded vigorously.

"I mean," she continued, "yes I am."

She put her hand on the doorframe, trying to stretch her arm out in a seductive manner. Her face looked like she'd just pulled a muscle.

"Well, SexBomb," he said, "thank you for wasting my time."

"I..."

"I'm going to report you to RuralHookupsRUs.com," he threatened. "VGL my ass. Whose photos were those anyway?"

He stormed away towards his car, and she started closing the front door.

"Are you crazy?" Devon demanded. "Sing!"

"Sing?"

"Sing him a frigging lullaby!" he cried, pushing her out the door. Understanding dawned on her. Devon covered his ears.

"*Rockabye baby...*" Liza began. The dude kept walking. "*On the tree top...*" His steps slowed. "*When the wind blows, the cradle will rock...*" He stumbled, arms flopping limply at his side. "*When the bough breaks, the cradle will fall...*" He fell to his knees, eyes rolling into the back of his head. "*And down will come baby...*" His cheek smacked into the paving stones of the driveway. "*...Cradle and all.*"

Devon came to her side, uncovering his ears. Liza stared at the fallen dude.

I did that, she thrilled, feeling a rush of invincibility.

"Come on," Devon said, "we've got to get LumberjackLuvsLife inside before your next date arrives."

"My next date?" Liza asked.

Devon shrugged.

"If you're going to make art, you need raw material."

Chapter 16

There was a clatter of dumbbells being foisted about in the basement of the Allstar residence—not an unusual noise in that particular abode, at least until Troy came down from his room and his parents looked up from their books, realizing the basement body-pumping was still underway.

"Who's lifting weights?" his mom asked.

"Is it that new friend of yours? Chad, was it? He certainly looks like he works out," his dad chuckled.

"Uh, yeah," Troy said.

He stomped down the wooden stairs and watched as Gibbie did arm curls with five forty-five-pound weights loaded onto either end of a barbell. He set it down and went to look at the cracked mirror Troy had set up there long ago. Gibbie wore a tank top and flexed his tiny biceps, his body as skinny as ever.

"Hey," Troy said.

Gibbie swirled around, blushing a deep red.

"I...uh..."

"It's okay," Troy said, "every guy flexes his muscles in the mirror now and then."

"Yeah, well, some guys have muscles to flex," Gibbie sighed.

"For someone who was the center of attention in the cafeteria yesterday, you seem kind of down," Troy said. He came and sat on the bench. Gibbie sat next to him.

"Yeah, it was pretty cool."

"You still pissed at me for raining on your parade?"

"Kind of." Then he shrugged. "No, not really. It was fun and all, but...look at me. I'm the strongest person on the planet, and I'm still the same skinny dork."

"It never used to bother you before that you were skinny," Troy said.

"It kind of did," Gibbie countered.

"So why didn't you do anything about it?"

"It felt kind of hopeless."

"And now?"

"Now," he sighed, "I know it's hopeless."

He picked up the most recent issue of *Muscle Pump* magazine. A bulging yet defined fitness model grinned back with a perfect smile.

"In order to gain muscle size one must take the muscle to failure," Gibbie read, and then, throwing down the magazine, "but my muscles don't get tired, so they're not going to grow."

Troy looked at his brother with fresh sympathy.

"There are other things in the world, you know."

"Kind of doesn't mean much coming from a guy with a body like yours."

"We could play that *Star Trek* game of yours. That always makes you feel better."

"That's kind of ruined too," Gibbie said. "Part of why I liked those games was because I got to make-believe that I was powerful. Now that I *am* powerful, I have to make-believe that I'm not. It sucks."

Troy felt the full intensity of his brother's situation.

"You know, if you really want to do the track team, then do the track team."

"I'm not sure how much fun it will be," Gibbie shrugged. "I already know I'll win. And the whole getting-up-at-6-a.m. thing gets tired pretty quick."

Troy patted him on the back.

"For what it's worth, I'm pretty sure Riley and Markham are going to leave you alone from now on."

"Yeah, that doesn't suck," Gibbie agreed. Then, as something occurred to him, he said, "Can I ask you something?"

"Shoot."

"How do you get someone to like you?"

It was the question every teen asked him or herself, sometimes every other minute. Troy thought about Jesse.

"I'm not sure. You do stuff together, I guess. If you laugh at the same things, start talking the same way, with little inside jokes, not annoying the hell out of each other too much...then I guess you start to like each other."

"Well, what if you want to get someone to like you in a...special way."

"Oh," Troy said, "a special way."

Troy thought of Jesse. Troy thought of Chad.

I've made such a mess, he thought, *I'm the last person to be giving advice.* But Gibbie's yearning gaze demanded an answer.

"You take a chance," Troy said at last, "and try not to screw it up."

Gibbie nodded. "Take a chance," he echoed.

"Just don't ask me how to get them to stay," Troy murmured.

"Flowers," Gibbie said.

Troy's head jerked up, but Gibbie was no longer paying attention to him.

"I think I'll start with flowers."

When Chad gazed out his bedroom window that particular evening, the sun was lowering on the horizon. He turned on his cat eyes to get a better look at what appeared to be a hunk on his bike coming down the street.

"Troy," he whispered.

Quickly, Chad looked in the mirror, tried on three different T-shirts, and put fresh product in his hair. He then went running down the stairs.

There came a loud knock on the door.

"Got it!" he yelled to his dad.

Heart hammering, he yanked on the handle and tried to look nonchalant.

"Hey, Chad."

"Gibbie?"

The younger of the Allstar brothers held a bouquet of roses. He wore a blue suit that was at least a size too big. Troy was nowhere to be seen, but Chad could swear his scent was on the wind.

Gibbie held the flowers towards the male cheerleader.

"I love you, Chad," Gibbie said. "I've loved you for as long as I can remember."

Please don't, Chad thought, choking back the words. To his own surprise, he had tears in his eyes. *And where's Troy?* he wondered.

"I would be honored," Gibbie said as Chad reluctantly took the flowers from his outstretched hands, "and very pleased, if you would go on a date with me."

Chad stared into those eyes, magnified by a pair of thick glasses, blinking up at him with so much hope.

"Gibbie, I..." he struggled, "I'm very flattered."

The little strongman beamed, and Chad realized this was the first time Gibbie had ever asked anyone out. He'd never heard the "I'm very flattered" lead-up before. He didn't know what it heralded.

Chad bit his lip, looked away, and then forced himself to continue.

"Gibbie, I think of you as more of a little brother. We can still go do something—see a movie, grab a burger, but..."

Understanding crept onto Gibbie's face.

"But it won't be a date, will it?"

"No, Gibbie, it won't," Chad agreed.

From behind a tree, Troy watched Gibbie in his ill-fitting suit. He felt Gibbie's excitement as he walked up to Chad's door. He could feel Chad's excitement as he opened it. Troy hopped back on his bike and pedaled away as the sun began to set, not sticking around for how the rest turned out.

Chapter 17

The following morning Liza went about her new routine, rising several hours before school started. There was much to be done. Not about the house—though heavens knew Mrs. Dedarling would have fretted to no end watching the dust build up on her vast collection of paintings and sculptures. But such matters were trifling in the face of what it took to maintain *true* art—a two-person job, as it turned out.

In the center of the upstairs art studio, the sole focus of Liza and Devon's combined attention, were five naked men, all of them young and muscular. Their joints were merged together, one man kneeling on one leg, his flesh fused to the floor where they met, another man's arms clasped through his, leaning on his back in a pose stolen from Cirque du Soleil. They, too, were fused together. In fact all five men were attached to each other in some fashion or another.

Two of them were cheek to cheek—quite literally, their skin and the bones of their jaws merged together. Another man seemed to be falling, but hands from one of the cheeky fellows—as Liza had come to call them—had his arms behind him, fists melded into the falling man's rear, so that he simply tilted at a dangerous angle. The soles of his feet rested on the same cheeky man's thighs, as if he were a swimmer ready to push off from a wall. Liza had cooed and made him flex his arms into the double-biceps pose, and then Devon squeezed his fingers into the shoulders, elbows, and wrists, twisting around ligaments, locking him in place.

"I wonder if I could turn their heads around backwards," Devon mused.

One of the cheeky men began to whimper.

Liza went to him, dabbing at his tears with a hankie.

"There, there, don't cry," she said. His online handle had been Karl_the_Kuddler. That was before he'd become part of the Creation. "If you don't stop crying, Devon will have to *make* you stop."

Looking down, Karl_the_Kuddler saw that the man fused to him no longer had a mouth. It was just a lump of flesh.

"Please," he begged.

"What did I say?" she pressed, talking to him as if he were a petulant toaster. She squeezed shaving cream into her palm, humming to herself contentedly as she spread it across his cheeks. With a new razor she scraped the scruff from his jaws. There was something therapeutic about the task, and the fact that she and Devon were doing this together made her glow. Creating and maintaining the creature gave her a feeling of purpose and connection unlike any she'd ever known.

She bustled busily, and she no longer needed the jeweler's glass to see the Creation for what it was. An object. She stepped back to regard it as a whole, imagining what pieces they would add to it next.

"So I was thinking," Liza said, patting on aftershave, "when are we going to add some women to the Creation?"

"I told you," Devon sighed, "this piece is all about male energy."

"Sounds kind of gay," Liza said. She tried, and failed, to keep her tone nonchalant.

Silence reigned in the room for a moment and Liza tried to ignore the flush rising to her cheeks. Devon applied shaving cream to one of ten muscular thighs belonging to the Creation.

"If you have something to say, just say it."

She looked at the Creation, and then to him.

"Mandy says that everyone who's gotten powers is a homo," Liza said in a rush. And then, with a tremble to her voice, "So, is there something you want to tell me?"

Devon took a deep breath.

"Actually, there is. Wow, after holding this inside for so many years, imagining what this moment would be like, and now here it is. No more lying, no more hiding the real me. Liza..."

"Yes, Devon?"

"Mandy's an idiot. She's a ditzy cheerleading shopaholic, okay?"

Liza flopped her hands.

"It's just..."

"Yes?"

She bit her lip. She'd had the balls to come this far, but now the stakes grew in her mind. What if Devon was gay? What then? Did it actually matter? He loved her; wasn't that enough?

"Look," he continued, "are you a dyke?"

"No!"

"Exactly," he said.

She considered pointing out that although he claimed they were soulmates, they'd barely even made out. But before she could...

"I love you, babe," he said. And that settled it.

"I love you too," she replied, the words bringing a glow to her cheeks.

"Oh, I almost forgot," Devon added, his hypnotic eyes gleaming with excitement. "Look what I picked up."

He pulled a plastic bottle from his back pocket.

"Baby oil," he said with a devilish grin.

Hope grew in Liza's heart.

"That'll be fun later," she said seductively.

"Later?" Devon scoffed. "Right now."

"Mr. Impatient," she said, starting to unbutton her red blouse, which she'd pilfered from Mrs. Dedarling's closet. She felt stupid now for doubting him. He'd been planning to seduce her all along, the little devil. Except Devon had already turned his attention back to the Creation, wiping the excess foam off Luvs_2_Sing's now smooth legs. Devon then squirted baby oil into his hands and began rubbing it into the Creation's silky skin, giving the hard muscles a polished gleam.

Liza bit her lip and began to do her shirt back up.

Chapter 18

Dear Diary,

Things are getting drama-rrific! Hold on to your ink or you're going to give yourself a skid mark! Mandy Candy has not only dyked out—she's...

The bell rang, heralding the end of the school day, and there was the usual scramble amongst upper- and lower-classmen alike, rushing to get home.

"I just don't know what to do about this Gibbie thing," Chad said to Mandy as they packed their bags at their lockers.

"Well, it sounds to me like you have a blocked fourth chakra," Mandy replied.

"Come again?"

"Chad, you really should come to this consciousness-raising yoga class I'm in. I only caught the last ten minutes of it this morning, but it's really changed my outlook on things. Let me ask you this. How's your heart doing?"

"Not so good," he replied.

She nodded knowingly.

"Dear sweet Chad. You have major issues. Your mom died when you were a kid. Your father denies you affection. Jake left you. And Troy, well, let's not go there. You finally have the chance to be loved, but you think you don't deserve it. So you go after guys who are like your father, distant and unavailable."

"You got all that out of a ten-minute yoga class?"

She gripped his smooth forearm.

"Listen, I'd love to chat more, but if I hurry, I can catch the tail end of this breath workshop over at the Y."

"Okay, call me after."

"Can't," she winced. "I've got a potluck with the grrrls from the vegan drop-in center. Later, babe!"

He watched her go.

"What about cheerleading practice?" he shouted, but she was already gone.

He shook his head. Could she be right? He tried to picture kissing Gibbie. Chad's mouth instantly soured up. All the same, he did not go right to cheerleading practice. Instead he roamed the emptying halls like the predator that he was. His nose flexed in and out and his ears sharpened into points.

"Your antimatter is mine," he heard Gibbie's voice cry.

Chad hurried over to the closed door it had come through. He opened it without hesitation. Gibbie sat there with a couple of other geeks, throwing an octagonal die onto a board filled with miniature soldiers.

"What do you want?" Gibbie demanded as soon as he spotted Chad.

"Can we talk?" the cheerleader asked.

"Make it quick," the small boy grunted. "Some of us have a life."

The cheerleader winced at the bitterness.

He sounds like Mandy and me.

Gibbie joined him in the hall, and went immediately over to the fountain to refill his water bottle.

"I'm really sorry for what happened the other night," Chad said.

The water from the fountain came out in a pitiful gurgle.

"Thank you for the apology," Gibbe said, screwing the lid on the bottle. It was barely a quarter-full.

"That's it?" Chad said, jumping in Gibbie's way.

Gibbie easily picked him up and moved him out of the way.

"Yes, Chad, that's it."

Chad followed the younger student to the classroom door.

"We can still be..."

"What?" Gibbie demanded, rounding on him. "Friends? I have friends, Chad. Real ones. I don't need a cheerleader in my circle, okay? Do you think I'm stupid enough to believe you'd actually invite me to anything? That we'd hang out?"

"We do hang out," Chad replied.

"Not anymore," Gibbie snapped. "You think I'm a joke, and the fact that I can lift heavy things hasn't changed that."

"Maybe with a makeover," Chad offered, trying to lighten the mood the way he would with Mandy. Gibbie's face turned red.

"If you'll excuse me, I have to get back to where I belong. You should too."

The door clicked shut behind him.

"So," Mandy said excitedly to Liza as they stood by Mandy's yellow VW, "you totally have to come to this breathing workshop with me."

"I already know how to breathe," Liza replied. "I do it all the time."

Mandy contemplated this.

"Good point. So do I. Okay then, how about this. Let's reclaim our female essences from the patriarchal hegemony!"

"Uh, sure." It was as good a way as any to avoid going back to the Dedarling mansion.

"Great. Let's go shopping!"

Moments later at the mall...

"This is very you," Mandy said to Liza, holding up a satin dress that was five sizes too small for the tall girl. A chunk of the mall was still cordoned off with yellow police tape, but Mandy's favorite store, Little Miss Thing, was having a red tag sale.

"I'm not sure," Liza said. She was thinking about Devon. All day long, he haunted her thoughts. She hated that they'd fought. She hated it even more that he was lying to her. But the thought of being alone again, after finally knowing what it was like to have someone...

"Well, at least try it on," Mandy insisted.

Liza looked to the shopkeeper for help, but the mid-forties woman was thin as a rake and looked upon this Amazon and her punked-out friend in horror.

"Fine," Liza said, flipping through the rack and pulling out a much larger version of the same dress. "But *this* is my size."

"You tell 'em, grrrl," Mandy growled. "The personal *is* political."

When Liza emerged from the change room, Mandy had to give it to her. In that dress, Liza was in her buxom glory.

"I feel like I'm about to fall out," Liza said, preparing to retreat behind the curtain.

"No way," Mandy said, pulling her back in front of the mirror. "You look amazing. Guys like a girl with a nice rack."

"Guys?" Liza asked.

"Oh, I meant chicks. Lesbos," Mandy rumbled. "My Goddess, it's tough getting over this heterosexist brainwashing."

Liza nodded and continued to ponder the dress in the mirror.

"It's not very bulldyke," she said, deciding to play along with Mandy.

"Pshaw." Mandy waved her words away. "It's totally WeHo *L-Word* chic."

And then, losing her persona for a moment, in a more down-to-earth tone she said, "You look good. That's all that matters."

The compliment was sincere and totally took Liza off-guard. She regarded Mandy differently. For just a second it actually felt like they were friends.

"Mandy, have you ever liked someone, and they liked you back, but you knew that they were keeping things from you?"

"Oh my Goddess, are you talking about Sherry from chemistry class?" Mandy squealed. "You so have a crush on her, don't you? I hear she's totally bi-curious!"

"Um, yeah, okay," Liza replied, regretting her momentary attempt to open up.

Mandy just kept feeling the fabric of Liza's dress.

"You could try one on," Liza offered.

Mandy pulled her hand back as if stung.

"No. I'm fine. I'm the butch," she smiled and, with a false laugh added, "Save the role-playing for the bedroom, sister."

"Well, it looks like you were right about the guys liking it," Liza said, just as glad to change the topic.

Mandy looked over her shoulder at a teen in a football jacket staring in from the store's entrance.

"Evan Mueller," Mandy blushed. "Now he is one cute..."—she caught herself—"...miserable son of a bitch. Can you believe him? Staring at us because we're a couple of dykes. You know what? I'm not putting up with it."

She looked ready to march up to him when Liza pulled her back.

"Mandy?"

"What?"

"Why are you doing this?"

"Doing what?"

"Hanging out with me."

"Because that's what lesbian best friends do."

Liza was beginning to understand why the closet was so exhausting. Devon wouldn't come out, Mandy refused to go back in, and Liza's own charade was quickly wearing thin.

"Are you sure you're a lesbian?" Liza finally asked.

"Am I sure," Mandy practically spat. "Would I have quit cheerleading if I wasn't sure?"

"About that," Liza replied, "you do realize you can be a lesbian *and* a cheerleader. There's even a movie about it."

"I...well..." Mandy looked about as if she were going to be sick as she processed this new and unexpected information.

"Mandy, have you ever even *been* with a woman?"

The panic was full in Mandy's eyes, and she immediately went on the defensive.

"If you're finished bashing my sexuality, I have to go change my non-bleached hemp menstrual pad," she snapped. Marching away, she added over her shoulder, "It's a life*style*, not a life!"

Liza watched her storm off to the restroom.

"She's right, you know," a male voice said.

She turned, and Evan Mueller, curly-haired football stud, stood there.

"About what?" Liza demanded.

"You do look pretty."

"You're funny," she replied, clearly not laughing.

"Why would that be a joke?" Evan asked.

She looked down at herself and back at him.

"You should go before my friend gets back."

"Sure," he said, "I just wanted to give you this."

She took a slip of paper from his outstretched hand.

"It's my phone number," he explained, "so you can call me, and we can go on a date."

Liza regarded it suspiciously.

"If this is the number for Pizzaville..."

"Liza! You're hot, okay? I'm just glad you're finally at a point where you're ready to show it off," Evan insisted. "Just one more thing."

"Yeah?" She waited for the bomb to drop, for him to call her an ogre, or lard-ass, or ask how the oxygen was at her altitude.

Instead he reached up and gently placed her hair behind her ears.

"Better," he said. "Now I can see your face."

Liza tried to say something, but found that as powerful as her voice was, it was mute in the face of this tall, dark, and handsome young man.

As he left the store he turned and mouthed the words "call me" while making a phone gesture with his thumb and pinky finger next to his ear. She waved shyly.

"What did that jerk want," Mandy demanded, popping back into view.

"Nothing," Liza lied.

"So what do you think?" Mandy asked. "About the dress?"

"I think," Liza began, "I think I'll take it."

Mandy clapped excitedly as Liza returned to the change room. With the curtain closed, safely hidden from Mandy's view, Liza looked at Evan's number. She folded it like an origami master, and tucked it between her breasts.

Chapter 19

Devon heard the door open and for just a moment he waited for the clickity-clack of his mother's heels and her usual spewing babble.

I killed her, he reminded himself as he sat in front of his new computer. His chest tightened, but the regret was transitory, fading behind a wall of ennui.

Liza walked into the room. She held a fancy-looking shopping bag. His mom would've approved. He stared at his video monitor.

"You didn't make it to school today," she said.

"Busy," he replied. "Did you bring food?"

"No," she said, "I didn't. I got a new dress, though. Want to see me in it?"

"Can I eat it?" he asked.

"No," she replied, "you can't eat it."

"Then I don't want to see it."

She walked over to where Devon gazed at his monitor. She was pretty sure she knew what he'd be watching. The Creation slept fitfully. Devon had taken to drugging it when she wasn't around to sing to it.

Over Devon's shoulder she watched the video of Jesse and Troy in the locker room. On the floor next to Devon was the bottle of baby oil.

"Do you mind if I delete this?" she asked, reaching towards the keyboard.

He smacked her hand back.

"Ow!"

"Why would we delete it?" he scoffed.

"Well, you've seen it a hundred times already."

Probably more, she refrained from saying.

"Have you even sent it to Troy and Jesse?" she pressed. "To the football team? To YouTube?"

He said nothing.

"This is my favorite part," he giggled.

Jesse licked Troy's nipple. Devon writhed in delight.

"No pretending you're not a fag after that," he sneered.

"I suppose not," Liza said quietly, drawing herself to her full height and stepping back.

She regarded Devon, and then the Creation. It was surrounded by cat litter. It reeked. Surely a relationship had more to offer than this.

From between her breasts, she pulled out Evan's phone number. She considered it for a moment, tucking it safely away again. She was tired of Devon, tired of his Creation, and, most importantly, she was tired of being Lezzie Liza. In that moment, her mind was made up.

"You and your boyfriends have fun," she said to Devon, turning and walking away.

Over his shoulder, still not looking away from the monitor, he yelled, "You've got another date tonight!"

Patting her bosom she muttered to herself, "Yes I do."

It was well past midnight when a jet-black pickup truck pulled into Liza's driveway. She watched Evan's hand guiding the wheel with strength and confidence. The beast of a vehicle grumbled to a halt, and he cut the engine. They sat there for a moment, silently watching the buzz of mosquitoes diving into the insect zapper hanging from the sagging awning. He looked at her, and Liza's breathing quickened. He leaned over and they made out—for the fifth time that night! His tongue was rough and clumsy, but she didn't care. It made her feel desirable.

He pulled back and smiled at her mischievously.

"So you going to invite me in?" he asked.

She looked to her dilapidated house. Her aunt's house, actually.

"That's strange," Liza said, her brow furrowed.

"What?" Evan said, sliding his fingers under her dress. She let him work his way half up her thigh before smacking his hand.

"The TV's on," she said.

"Maybe you forgot to switch it off," he said.

She shook her head.

"Someone's in there, on the couch."

Evan's body tensed all over.

"I'll go check it out," he said.

"No! My aunt must have called in sick for her overnight shift," Liza lied. "Now probably isn't the best time to meet her."

"That's cool," he whispered, nuzzling her neck, "I know somewhere else we can go."

She reluctantly pushed him back.

"I really have to go check on my aunt," she said, about to get out of the truck.

"Wait!" he said, hopping out and rushing around to open Liza's door.

"My Lady," he said, taking her fingers and helping her down. It made her heart race. Finally! He moved in with his tongue aimed at her mouth, and she was careful to keep her lips closed. The poor boy had no idea how much danger he was in.

"I don't want my aunt to see," she explained.

"I had a real nice time tonight, Liza," he said.

"Me too," she beamed.

She stared at his strong shoulders in his letterman's jacket as he got back in his rig, and waved as the truck pulled away. Her smile quickly cracked when the headlights disappeared down the street.

She marched for the front door. There was no need to unlock it. The handle and lock had been reduced to metallic putty, and the door itself stood ajar.

"Devon!" she called, stepping inside.

From the hall she had a clear view of the couch, but it was now deserted. The TV played black and white reruns of *The Addams Family*.

She took a tremulous breath.

"Devon?" she called. The entire house shook from the force of her voice.

She opened her mouth a third time, and a hand closed tight around it.

"Now, now, Liza," he said, "we wouldn't want you waking the neighbors."

Liza's breathing grew hard. He was going to kill her, probably do to her what he'd done to his own mother. What would it feel like to be permanently melded to the couch, where she spent so much of her time, the remote merged with her hand forevermore? She waited for his fingers to sink into her, but instead he shoved her into a chair.

"I was worried sick about you," he spat. "You just go out and don't come back? I tried calling..."

Liza tried to process the fact that she was still alive, and that Devon actually sounded like he cared.

"My cell was turned off," Liza said, trying to sound defiant.

"I noticed. And for what? To go out with some dickhead jock?"

"He's not a dickhead," Liza said. "*He* pays attention to me."

"I pay attention to you."

"He likes my body."

Devon opened his mouth and snapped it shut.

"You need to come home," he growled.

"I am home," Liza countered, "Or hadn't you noticed?"

"This dump?"

"Yes," she said. "Not all of us come from money. How are the mortgage payments going on Mummy's house, by the way?"

"Yeah," he muttered, "like this place is paid off."

"Actually," she said, "it is."

"So this is it." He waved around. "This is what you want your life to be like? Dating some lame jock who's going to get old and fat, probably turn into a drunk, your ankle chained to the stove as you pop out a couple of kids?"

"I'd like to have a baby, actually."

"That is such a frigging cliché," he shouted. "Liza, this isn't you."

"You never bothered to find out who I actually am," she yelled. The force made Devon stagger back a step. "I like Evan," she continued. "He likes me. And I have friends, too, real friends."

"What, like Mandy, who thinks you're a dyke? Or Chad, who's buffed himself to such a shine you can see your reflection in his pecs?"

"You don't know them the way I do," she replied, her nose raised haughtily, though truth be told she'd barely spoken to the boys, and he had a point about Mandy. But Evan, Evan had never done her wrong. Devon, on the other hand...

"You can't be serious," he scoffed. "The whole point of you hanging out with them was to gather information, and instead you what? Learn some bull crap moral lesson?"

"It's done, Devon," she said, outwardly calm even if inside she trembled at the finality of this decision. "We're done. I don't want to be part of your twisted, lonely life."

"Just like that?" he huffed. "After everything we've done to-gether? Everything we've shared?"

"Devon, just go."

"I don't think so."

He ran at her, hands extended.

She let go a demonic shriek. The sound wave sent the TV smashing into the wall and Devon flew backwards, crashing into the front closet. The clothes rail fell on top of him, burying him under a worn winter jacket, along with a few overalls with the name Madge stenciled on the front breast pocket.

"Get out," Liza ordered. "And if you ever try to lay one of those hands on me again, I'll scream so hard your head will pop."

"You need me, Liza," he protested.

She opened her mouth threateningly and he scuttled out the door. Liza looked at what was left of the door handle. It was mash from Devon's touch.

What if he comes back while I'm sleeping?

She grabbed her keys from where she'd dropped them and went out to her aunt's old pickup truck. Ten minutes later it was pulling in behind a yellow VW Bug. Mandy nearly exploded with glee when she opened the door.

"I *knew* you'd be back," she cried. She grabbed Liza's hand and dragged her upstairs to the bedroom, prattling the entire time, "I have got the best hemp granola recipe *ever!* We are totally play-ing Martha tonight."

"Mandy, this is serious," Liza said as they sat on the bed.

"Oh my Goddess," Mandy said, "are you allergic to hemp?"

"Mandy!" Liza snapped, making the entire room shake.

After everything that had happened that night, Liza desperately needed a friend, an *actual* friend, one she could really talk to, and she was tired of playing lesbian wet nurse. Before that damn bottle of Etienne water she didn't speak to anybody about anything, but now that she'd gotten used to opening up to Devon, everything just wanted to spill out. No wonder people were constantly vomiting up personal information.

"I've been keeping things from you," Liza said, "and I can't anymore. You know that guy Devon in our class?"

"Yeah, yeah, vampire guy."

"Right," Liza agreed. "Well..."

"Shh," Mandy said, holding her finger up to Liza's lip, "not another word. I get it. I've seen you guys talking on the sly."

"You have?" Liza asked.

"Liza, I can turn invisible. I know what's going on."

"You do?" The thought filled Liza with horror. Who else knew? The police?

"Liza," Mandy sighed, "you were experimenting. I get it."

Liza thought of the Creation; an experiment indeed.

"You don't think it's weird?" Liza asked.

"It would be weird if you didn't experiment," Mandy assured her. "I mean, being a lesbian, wow! Not exactly something you turn your back on. So you wanted to be sure. You fooled around with Devon. No big. I saw *Chasing Amy.*"

"Mandy, I'm not talking about..."

Liza's words cut off. She looked down. Mandy was stroking her thigh.

"I've been thinking about what you said at the mall today," Mandy explained, her fingers inching their way up Liza's skirt. "And you're right. I've never been with a woman. So if I'm going to do this lesbian thing, then I've really got to *do* it."

Her nail hooked under Liza's underwear.

"Oh God," Liza cursed in panic.

"Goddess," Mandy corrected. Her other hand began to clumsily caress Liza's breasts.

"You don't have to be coy anymore," Mandy said. "Our love dares speak its name."

Liza did the only thing she could think to do. She began to sing.

"Hush little baby, don't say a..."

Mandy lurched forward, her mouth swallowing Liza's, choking the melody away with a full-on lesbo kiss.

Chapter 20

The next morning at school, Liza was pulling her geometry textbook from her locker when she was suddenly grabbed from behind. She panicked, and readied to blast Devon with her voice before he could unleash his power on her.

She stared into Evan's face and clamped her mouth shut.

"You okay?" he asked.

"You scared me," she choked.

"You haven't answered my text messages," he said.

"I've been busy?" she replied uncertainly.

"Well, un-busy yourself. We've got a game tonight. You should be there to cheer me on," he said. His hand brushed her thigh ever so slightly.

"I...I don't have anyone to sit with," she said nervously.

"Sit with your pal Mandy," he said as Mandy stopped next to the pair.

"Is this jerk bothering you?" Mandy asked.

He kissed Liza on the cheek. "Gotta go! Remedial English calls."

Mandy planted her hand on her hip.

"He just won't give up. As soon as some guys see a pair of dykes together, all they can think is threesome."

"Listen, there's something I need to tell you," Liza said.

"Yes, there is," Mandy said. "Why'd you take off this morning? I got out of the shower and you were gone. I was worried sick."

"I've been getting that a lot lately," Liza said. "It's just..."

"You freaked, after we..." Mandy rolled her eyes and then gave a wink. "It's cool. I was a little weirded out myself. I mean, wow! Talk about female energy."

"Yeah, not really what I wanted to chat about."

"Best not to ruin it with words," Mandy nodded. "It's too pure."

"Sure," Liza agreed. "So, tonight—I know you quit cheerleading and all, but do you want to go to the game with me?"

"Yes!" Mandy replied, just a little too excitedly. "I mean, whatever."

"Great. And there's one other tiny little thing," Liza said. "I'm not a dyke."

"We've been over this..." Mandy shook her head.

"I'm into Evan," Liza pressed. "He's into me. And for the record, he's not looking for a threesome. You're not his type."

Mandy struggled for something to say.

"See you at the game tonight!" Liza said brightly, sauntering away.

Chad Lenwick stood outside.

"I can't believe it's come to this," he said.

His feet teetered over the edge of a stone wall, ready to take the plunge of no return. The wind gusted up from below. He had no one. Not his father, not Troy, not Mandy, not even little Gibbie. This was it. He felt a faint wave of vertigo from the oblivion waiting at the bottom of this inevitable fall.

"Chad!"

It was Mandy. She always knew when he was teetering on the verge.

"Don't do it!" she begged.

He turned around and saw her running out a door and towards him as fast as she could. This was their favorite hangout place— the view was amazing—so of course she'd known where to find him. His only surprise was that she'd want to find him at all. And yet she jumped fearlessly onto the wall where he stood and grabbed his arm.

"I have to," he said. "It's the only way."

Together they stared at the triple chocolate cookie he held in his hand.

"I just can't take the loneliness anymore."

"It's going to be okay," she said. "Just put the cookie down, okay? It's not worth it. Let's take this nice and easy. I'm just going to put my fingers on the cookie, see? Now on the count of three, I want you to let go of the cookie. One..."

"Oh, just take it," he said, letting it go and hopping the two feet to the ground. "I've got another one in my backpack."

The rugby team from the nearby college jogged past. The view from here was not just fine—it was *damn* fine.

She took a ravenous bite and, with her mouth full, she said, "We have to find Gibbie."

"I don't think he wants to see me right now," Chad countered. "Besides, you dumped me, quit cheerleading, and now you're eating carbs. I don't even know you anymore."

She grabbed him by the collar of his pink polo and yanked on it.

"Find him!" she ordered.

He smiled and hugged her tight.

"My Mandy is back!"

At that particular moment Gibbie sat on a stool in chemistry class, drawing a picture of Chad while liquid bubbled in a beaker on the Bunsen burner in front of him. He drew a monstrous metal hunter's trap around Chad's head, ready to chomp shut. He admired his work until the pencil was pulled out of his fingers. It hung in the air before him, and then began to write, all on its own, next to the image of Chad. It then set itself back into Gibbie's flexed fingers.

He gazed down at what it had written: *"Hallway, now!"*

"Is something the matter, Mr. Allstar?" his teacher asked.

"I, uh..." He looked back down at Mandy's bubbly handwriting. "I really need to go to the restroom."

"Well, turn your Bunsen burner down first."

His beaker of orange fluid had started to boil over.

Outside the classroom, Gibbie took one look at Chad and appeared ready to go right back inside. He bounced off of Liza's force field.

"Sorry," she said, extending her hand and helping him up.

"Chad, I told you...," Gibbie began.

"This ain't about me, girlfriend," he said. "Talk to inviso-girl over there."

"What?" he said to Mandy.

"Wow, you weren't kidding. He has gotten bitchy," Mandy said.

"And you've gotten dikey," he replied.

"Snap," Chad said under his breath.

"Actually," Mandy said, "that's what I wanted to talk to you about. Remember when you said there might be other stuff that we all have in common, and that's why the water affected us the way it did?"

"Well, it was actually the fluoride isotope *in* the water, but yeah."

"Could..." She took a deep breath. "Could sexual orientation be one of those factors? I mean, you're gay, Chad's gay, Liza's a dyke, right?"

"I thought she was dating Evan from the football team," Gibbie replied.

"How did I go from the first to know everything to the last?" Mandy sighed.

"Look," Gibbie sighed. "First of all, my big brother's not gay, okay? He's the straightest guy I know."

Chad and Mandy looked to each other knowingly.

"And even if he were, that doesn't mean Liza's a lesbian. Gay men's brains and straight women's brains have similarities that straight guys and lesbians don't. If you were right about this whole sexual orientation correlation, my guess is that the guys who were affected would be gay, and the women would be straight. Now, if you'll please excuse me."

He gave them a dirty look and went back into class.

Mandy looked ready to cry. "Did he just say what I think he said?"

Chad nodded.

"You *are* straight!" he said, hopping up and down while clapping excitedly.

She grabbed him by the arm and dragged him down the hallway.

"I quit cheerleading. I cut my hair. I pierced my nose!"

"Yeah," Chad winced, then tried to find a silver lining. "Look on the bright side, at least you and Liza never made out, right?"

His eyes opened in shock at the look of horror on Mandy's face.

"*Never* speak of this ever again!" she snapped.

Chapter 21

Troy wasn't entirely sure why he was even bothering to show up for the game that night. There was no way he was making it off the bench. In fact, he was surprised Jesse hadn't had him cut from the team by now. For that matter, he was still trying to figure out why he hadn't quit.

Because I love him.

He took the thought, folded it carefully, placed it in a mail slot in his mind, and locked it away.

Doesn't mean it's not there.

He pushed open the door to the locker room, shifting his focus to the bag of gear slung over his back. The weight put a kink in his neck. It was a welcome distraction, but only for a moment. His brooding thoughts turned quickly to Chad, the feel of his skin, his infectious laugh, and his utter fierceness.

Why can't I be okay with being gay? Troy wondered.

His stomach still turned at the word, and as he pushed his way into the locker room he felt at an all-time low. He tried to lock the sentiment down, cage it behind the barrier in his mind, but before he could, a wave of foreboding pulled his head up from his reverie. Something was up—he sensed it even before he saw the guys, scattered about the locker room.

Their emotions swept into him, a unified force of worry, dread, and foreboding.

When they saw him, there was momentary hope.

They want me to play! he cheered to himself.

"Is Jesse with you?" the coach asked.

"No," Troy replied. "Haven't seen him for hours."

"No one has," the coach snorted, "and he's not answering his cell."

Adam, a stocky quarterback, banged his head into his helmet.

"We're screwed."

Coach kicked a garbage can.

Troy felt their morale drop like lead weights, dragging him down.

"We might as well just forfeit," Adam scowled.

There were nods and grunts of agreement. Coach Lenwick glowered at their inevitable defeat. Troy swallowed a lump in his throat. They all had reason to be down, but he couldn't help but wonder at how quickly they'd given up. It was almost as if they were mirroring his own internal state.

"So that's it?"

It was Chad who spoke. There was an audible creak of necks twisting towards him. He stood off to the side in his shiny short shorts and tight sleeveless shirt. His pompons rustled in the silence. Troy could feel Chad's own doubt, but the difference between him and everyone else in the room was that Chad knew all about doubt, but he'd decided long ago that the cost of giving in to it was too high.

"You're just going to give up?" he pressed.

"No offense, Chaz..." Adam began.

"Chad," he corrected.

"Right. You ever played football?"

"No."

"Then you might want to shut it right about now."

The entire team glared at the only cheerleader in the room. They didn't even try to hide their revulsion. He held his pompoms awkwardly, looking to his dad for support. The coach shook his head with disgust.

"This isn't cheerleading," the elder Lenwick snapped. "We're here to win, and to do that, we need our star player."

"We're all star players."

Troy wondered who had the balls to speak up. Everyone looked at him, and he realized the words had issued from his own mouth.

"Oh, um..." He looked to Chad for support. He appeared ready to say something, but a harsh look from his dad and the blond's mouth snapped shut.

Troy sought help from the guys. They just kept staring at him.

"Adam!" he said to the guy who'd dissed Chad. "Two games ago you scored the winning touchdown."

He felt a surge of pride from Adam. That helped bolster Troy, and as he felt his insides strengthen, that resolve spread outwards. There were nods of agreement from the other guys. Their doubt loomed, but behind it, a desire to believe. "Riley," he continued, "last time I checked, you were the biggest, toughest brick house around. Nobody on the field messes with you, right?"

From the corner of his eye Troy caught Chad giving him the thumbs-up.

"Hell's yeah," Riley said, "and Markham's the fastest dawg we got."

"Damn straight," Markham agreed.

"See, guys!" Troy said. "We're awesome."

And they were—they could feel it. To Troy it was like a warm light filling the room. Even Chad felt his chest swelling with pride.

"Coach, I think with a few tweaks your game plan can still work," Troy said.

"Yeah?" the coach asked, still a hint of reserve left in him, but Troy could sense, beneath the doubt, a flicker of confidence, a desire for Troy to be right. The flame just needed to be fanned.

Troy looked to Chad, hoping for inspiration, and got it.

"Jesse's not the only one who can bring the game home," Troy said, his own resolve growing as he gazed into the cheerleader's blue eyes. "There are other really awesome players on the field, ones I would be honored to play with."

Chad blushed, and Troy gave him a daring wink.

The guys began to huddle around the former wrestler, staring at the board with their plays on it. Troy began pointing out a few adjustments, drawing quick lines with colored chalk.

Chad watched with growing admiration—and a lump in his throat.

As Troy concluded, there was a loud cheer from all the guys, and they began banging into each other, chest to chest.

"Come on, animals!" the coach cried, and they went packing out en masse.

Troy was the last to go, and he paused, turning to Chad.

"Thank you," Troy said.

"For what?"

"For speaking up. For not taking this lying down."

Chad shrugged. "It's what I do."

"I know," Troy agreed, "and I really..."

Love you for that.

"...like that about you."

Chad blushed.

"Don't you have a game to lead?"

Troy's eyebrows rose in slight surprise.

"Lead, eh?"

"Kind of looks that way," Chad pointed out.

"It's a pretty big change from the bench-warming plans I had all night," Troy said, and then, more shyly, his cheeks turning red, "Kiss me good luck?"

Now it was Chad's turn to look surprised.

"For serious?"

"Yeah," he said.

"What's changed?"

"We have," Troy said. "All of us. I know what you feel, for me, and...I feel it too."

Chad walked up to him. Troy rubbed his cheek. He was so damn pretty. Cupping Chad behind the neck, he drew the cheerleader to him. Their lips merged in moist warmness. They pulled apart.

"Thanks," Troy murmured, "I needed that."

Chad pushed him towards the field.

"Go get 'em, queero."

Chapter 22

Mandy and Liza walked towards the stands overlooking the high school's football field. A glare was etched on Mandy's face. Liza clutched her Big Gulp excitedly. She wore a T-shirt that bore an image of the Nuffim Marmot, and carried a rolled-up sign that read, *"Evan, Evan, he's my man, if he can't do me, no one can!"*

"This is my first football game," Liza said, slurping from her straw.

"Really? I didn't catch that the first 20 times you told me," Mandy snapped.

Liza didn't even hear.

"I can't wait to see Evan play, and then after the game he and I are driving up to Lovers' Lookout and..."

"Enough," Mandy said, holding her hand up for silence. "I said I'd come to the game, so I'm at the game. You can stop shoving your boyfriend in my face."

"I thought you'd be happy for me," Liza said.

"I am," Mandy replied. "Well, I'm trying to be. It would be easier if I hadn't given up everything for lady love only to discover I don't even like it."

The cheerleading squad was shouting away as the bleachers

filled up. Mandy moped as she gazed at the girls doing a routine she herself had choreographed. Liza, on the other hand, had noticed a figure in a dark coat heading away from everyone else, towards the school's locked doors instead of the football field. Her heart raced nervously.

"Mandy, you go ahead," she said.

"Sure," Mandy replied. She kept staring at the cheerleaders, doing flips, throwing each other into the air, everyone cheering them. Her shoulders sagged as her feet thudded up the stairs and joined the masses in the stands. She didn't watch as Liza stopped at the school doors.

"What are you doing here?"

Devon turned, hands raised towards Liza. She jumped back. He smirked and simply straightened his trench coat.

"Relax. I'm just here for the big game. Wanted to show my school spirit."

"You don't have any school spirit."

"And you do? Right, I forgot about the new and improved Liza. Kind of like you forgot about this."

He held up a piece of paper with Liza's handwriting on it.

It read, "Hit List. Homeroom."

She grabbed it from him and stuffed it into her purse.

"That was just...theoretical," she blurted out. "I was never actually going to..."

"Do to them what you did to my mom?" he interrupted.

"That was an accident," she snapped. "And I don't do stuff like that anymore."

"Then what are you doing talking to the likes of me?"

"I...I just wanted to warn you, not to try anything."

Only now did she notice how terrible he looked—skin like rice paper, a spatter of stubble on his cheeks, eyes bloodshot.

"Hey, maybe I'll come hang out with you and your friends after," he offered with a forced joviality. "I am one of the gang, after all." He wiggled his fingers for emphasis. "We could double date and get floats at the ice cream shop!"

"Enough," Liza snapped. "If you try to hurt any of us..."

"Why bother? I'm over you, and them..." He shrugged his head towards the field. "They're already in a hell of their own making."

"You're just so...so negative," she said with pity.

"Wow," he said, "you wear a couple of my mom's dresses and poof! you start to sound like her. You would've loved her. Too bad you killed her."

Her cheek trembled at his words, and for a moment she was the old Liza, with lots to say, but no voice with which to say it.

"Well, see ya," she finally mumbled, turning and walking away.

"Yeah," he said, "I'm pretty sure you will."

To himself he added, "And don't worry. I'm not going to hurt your friends. I'm going to leave that up to you. And I sure hope everybody enjoys the video you gave me."

"Are you okay?" Mandy asked as Liza maneuvered her bulk through the crowd of students and overly enthusiastic parents.

"Never better," Liza lied.

She scanned the field, searching for Evan, and keeping an eye out for Devon.

"We're pretty far up," Liza said. "Couldn't we move closer?"

"Are you here to spend time with me, or rub your boyfriend in my face?" Mandy demanded.

"Sorry," Liza muttered. Mandy was squinting to try to bring the cheerleaders into focus. Chad hoisted Tanya Delzowski to the top of the pyramid. She stood there proudly, and even did a high kick over her head. The crowd began to cheer, but the pyramid wobbled as Tanya lost her balance, and the whole bunch of them came crashing into each other.

"Idiot!" Mandy cursed. "Just because Tanya's team captain now does not mean she's got my moves. I should be down there."

"Okay!" Liza said, getting ready to move closer to the field.

"Sit," Mandy ordered, grabbing Liza and jerking her back into her seat before stuffing herself with popcorn.

"Wow, they are really getting clobbered," Mandy commented as the clock approached the twenty-minute mark. "The cheerleading squad really has its work cut out for it if the team wants to win. I'm not sure even we...I mean they... can raise spirits that high."

"Maybe if Evan saw me watching, that might inspire him," Liza offered.

"Oh please, honey, Evan's a B-list player at best," Mandy replied, getting up and stretching her arms. "I'm going to the ladies' room. You guard our spots."

Liza watched her go. She waited for a few moments and then grabbed all their stuff and began walking down the stairs, searching for empty seats nearer the field. When she got almost to the bottom, she spotted a couple of empty chairs behind a pole. They would have to do. She was excusing her way down the aisle when two girls stood up right in front of her and barred the way.

"Where do you think you're going, freak?"

"I think this bench has already reached its maximum weight allowance," the second girl added. "Go find yourself a nice ocean and then beach yourself."

It was Lacey and Stacey. Lacey wore a neck brace and her arm was in a sling. Stacey had two bandages on her forehead and hobbled on crutches.

"You've got a lot of nerve," Stacey said.

"I don't know what you're talking about," Liza lied.

"It's kind of weird that the earthquake sent us to the hospital, and you don't even have a scratch," Lacey said, giving Liza a push.

"Mandy wasn't hurt either," she countered.

"She's been hanging out with you. Clearly she's suffered major head trauma."

"And we don't like the way you're taking advantage of her."

Lacey lifted her mammoth cup of diet soda, turned it over, and poured its contents all over Liza's head.

"Marine mammals need to stay hydrated," she said. "I learned that at SeaWorld."

Liza stood there shaking, her skin prickling from the cold liquid running down the back of her shirt, ice cubes stuck to her neck.

She opened her mouth, the scream built, and this time she'd flay the skin right off their skinny little bodies. The reverberations came up from her lungs, setting her vocal cords to vibrating, and Stacey shoved a hot dog, bun and all, deep into Liza's throat. She choked on the mass, struggling to breathe. The scream recoiled inside her, making her entire body tremble.

Stacey raised a crutch and shoved the tip full into Liza's belly.

Liza crashed backwards, knocking over the popcorn vendor, her body tumbling down the stairs and onto the field. People stared, and laughed. Somebody helped her to her feet. It was Chad, but she didn't see. She just pushed him away, running and hiding behind the stands. She coughed up hot dog, and then stood there, leaning on her knees, panting and trying to catch her breath. Sticky pop dripped from her hair and into her eyes.

Mandy, she thought, dialing on her cellphone. She got voicemail.

"Where are you?" Liza said after the beep. "I really need a friend right..." Her words trailed off, her slack-jawed stare taking in the field. "...now." She clicked the phone shut and took a step towards the impossible.

She watched as Mandy was tossed high into the air, a bright blue wig cascading around her, her pompons spinning in the glare of a spotlight. The bleachers above Liza vibrated with cheers and stomping feet. She coughed in a cloud of falling dust.

Mandy clearly did not go to the washroom as she'd claimed. Instead she went right up to Chad (and the other girls) and said, "Get it together, bitches. You're a mess out there!"

"Listen, traitor," Tanya snapped, "I'm pretty queer-positive, but every once in a while I meet a homo who just needs to be bashed."

"First of all, you can suck it," Mandy replied. "Second of all, I'm not gay."

Chad pressed his palms together, stared skyward and mouthed the words "thank you."

"So what?" Tanya demanded of Chad. "You think we should let your little fruit fly back on the team?"

"It couldn't hurt," Chad replied.

"I don't think so."

"Listen, Tanya, we're totally biting it, and it's not your fault," Chad reasoned. "You had a week to bounce back from Mandy's defection. That may be enough time for the football team to get it together, but let's face it, this is cheerleading. And we need her. We...miss her."

The other girls were nodding. Tanya rolled her eyes.

"Fine! But I'm still squad captain, and you have a lot of making up to do."

Minutes later Mandy had donned a uniform and was being thrown in the air.

Liza watched and slunk away, cola sticking to her long hair. She found Evan with the other players, in a huddle on the side of the field, figuring out their next strategy. She tapped him on his bulky shoulder pads.

"I need to talk with you," she said after he turned around.

He looked confused.

"Right now? Baby, we're in the middle of a game."

Beyond him, Troy was giving firm instructions.

"Adam, go for No. 32's left knee. It's injured."

"How do you know?" Adam asked.

Because he can feel it, Liza thought, staring at her boyfriend.

"I read it in the paper," Troy lied.

"Something bad's happened," she said to Evan.

His gentle paw lifted her sopping hair, and wiped crumbs from her lips.

"I can see that. I'll take care of it. *After* the game."

"Riley, Nos. 53 and 45 seem to have it in for you," Troy said.

"He was macking on their girls at the Hog and Ho," Markham sniggered.

"I can take 'em," Riley grunted.

"Markham, use that mouth of yours. Egg them on, really get them after Riley," Troy said. "I need them to break formation."

"No problem," Markham answered.

"Evan," Liza sobbed, "I can't go back up there. They humiliated me!"

He put his arm around her and took a few steps away from his teammates.

"I know, and I'm sorry, and they'll pay, but right now I have a game to win."

"So what are you saying? That your stupid game, which you're *losing,* is more important to you than me?"

"Don't be like that," Evan replied. "You don't expect me to just walk away."

He stared at her silent response.

"Do you?" he pressed.

"Do you love me?" she asked.

"What?"

"I said," she hissed, "do you *love* me?"

"Liza, are you crazy? We've been on one date."

He turned and started walking back towards Troy and the others.

A flurry of emotions swept through Liza in that instant. Even Troy would've been hard-pressed to keep up. Hurt. Anger. Betrayal. And most biting, abandonment. Her eyes narrowed.

"Fuck that," she muttered, "I am *not* going to be treated this way."

Slowly she began to sing.

The last any of Evan Mueller's teammates saw of him—alive— was as he wandered off the field in a trance, following after Liza like she was the Pied Piper of Nuffim High.

Chapter 23

"Why aren't you on the field?" Coach Lenwick asked Troy as his fellow football players took up their positions.

"Because I can do more good here," Troy answered. He'd remained on the sidelines the entire game.

The guys hunched down, and Troy let his awareness expand, as he'd been doing all evening. He could feel his teammates. He sorted through them one by one, and put each of them in their own little cubicle in his head.

Adam, who was a miracle during practices, began to feel the dreaded pressure that always tripped him during game time. The ball came his way. Troy filled Adam's room with confidence. Adam caught the ball and ran fast.

Fatigue plagued Kevin. Troy helped him reach deeper than the lactic acid building in the tackler's legs and he rammed the linebacker about to nail Adam.

And then Troy began to feel the other team as well. He filled their rooms with doubt and weighed them down with exhaustion. A cornerback reached for Adam and tripped. A linebacker was about to blindside him, but a sixth sense (Troy) warned the spunky little player and he saw the danger from the corner of his eye just in time to sprint left. The linebacker landed on grass.

And this was Troy's pièce de résistance: Adam's surging jump that knocked over a defenseman and carried them both over the line.

By the final two minutes of the game, the scoreboard said it all. They were one touchdown away from taking the game.

Chad came up to Troy.

"I don't know what you're doing, meaning I totally know what you're doing, and you look exhausted, but you've only got two more minutes to go."

Troy shook his head.

"I can't."

"What do you mean?"

"I mean," Troy panted, "I can sense them out there, barely, but that's it. It's hazy. I'm tapped out, man."

Chad nodded.

"Well, you did good all the same. We can still win this."

"I just...," Troy began, "I wanted this so bad. If we lose..."

"Well then," Chad said, "how about you get that hot ass of yours onto the field, and make sure we don't."

The corner of Troy's lip took on a devilish crook.

"What?" Chad demanded.

"I have a better idea."

He pushed a helmet into Chad's stomach.

"You're up."

Chad held the helmet away from his body, as if he'd go into anaphylactic shock if he touched it much longer.

"What are you talking about?" he demanded.

"Listen up, everyone," Troy said, getting the guys to huddle around him. "We're down to the wire. You're all exhausted. We need some fresh blood on the field."

"Troy! Troy! Troy!" they began shouting.

"I was wondering why you were hanging back," Markham said. "Smart thinking, man."

There were nods of agreement all around. Troy held up his hand.

"Not just me," he said. "Him."

Troy pointed at Chad, who looked for a means of escape as the entire football team attempted to see who Troy meant.

The cheers died down as they noticed the football helmet in Chad's hand. Normally Troy would have reached out and filled them with feelings of trust, but it was like turning on a tap and getting only a drip. Riley and Markham stepped forward, and Troy knew it was game over. They'd never let Chad play.

"Troy's gotten us this far," Markham said. "I say we follow his lead."

"You heard the man," Riley said to Chad. "Suit up."

In moments, something more impossible than superpowered teens went down.

"I can't believe I'm doing this," Chad said, his head covered by a helmet, pads springing up from his shoulders, football pants digging into his crotch.

"Just think of it as a game of fetch," Troy said.

"I'm wearing someone else's cup."

The guys looked at Chad doubtfully. And then Markham began the chanting.

"Chad! Chad!"

Riley picked it up.

"Chad! Chad!"

Soon they were all bellowing his name.

What a pack of monsters, he thought. "My animals" is what his dad had often called them.

Chad looked to his father, the team's coach, hoping in this quarter at least someone would see sanity and pull the plug on this mad venture. The look on his dad's face was so different from the one Chad had grown up with, the one that would gaze at his nelly offspring and say, *You'll never be my son.* Today it contemplated Chad and said something else: *Maybe.*

"Okay, girlz," the cheerleader cried, "let's kick some ass!"

It was a victory unlike Nuffim—or any other high school—had ever seen. After all, Chad moved as no other player could. His touchdown propelled the Nuffim Marmots into the regional championships for the first time in ten years.

Since the beginning of high school, Chad had tossed cheerleaders into the air, his feet forever remaining earthbound except for the occasional backflip, and so he had no idea what it would feel like to have his legs scooped out from under him and be bounced safely upwards by so many strong hands—until he sat on the football team's shoulders, paraded before the screaming crowd.

"Chad, Chad, he's our man!" the cheerleaders—his cheerleaders— had led the crowd in crying. Mandy blew him a kiss.

He caught it, smacked his chest with it, and then pumped the air with his fist.

The guys spirited him away to the confines of the men's change room, where for once he was not gripped with dread. Tonight he was not a flaming outcast in the most male of dominions. Tonight, he was a star. They clasped his thighs, chanting in unison, "Chad! Chad! Chad!" in their deep, tribal way.

Riley and Markham were among the most enthusiastic.

So this is what it feels like to be one of the boys, he beamed in wonder.

He had to lie back in their arms to get through the doorway, and inside they set him feet first on a bench, so that he could stand and tower above them all. He didn't realize it, but they were also presenting him: to his dad.

They parted, and his pop stepped onto the bench next to his son. There were tears in the coach's eyes. To Chad's amazement, there were tears in his own as well. Not only that, but many of the guys were misty-eyed as they watched.

They love him, Chad realized, *and they're happy he finally gets to have the son he always wanted.*

The coach crushed Chad tight against him. The bear hug happened so quickly Chad struggled to hug back.

The coach...

My dad.

...gripped him by his shoulder pads.

"I can honestly say I've never seen anything like that. I mean, you held the ball in your mouth and ran on all fours!"

He'd had to rip off the mouth guard *and* keep his teeth from puncturing the ball's delicate flesh to pull that off.

"And when you vaulted over those guys, and pushed off their backs...I never thought I'd say it, but maybe the football team could learn a thing or two from the cheerleaders."

There was nervous laughter at that and as wonderful as Chad felt, his insides tightened.

I'm not one of them, he knew. *I'm just visiting.*

He heard a pop and there was a spray of alcohol-free champagne. Plastic cups were filled with bubbly and passed around.

"To my son, Chad," the coach said, "for scoring the final touchdown..."

More cheers.

"...and to Troy. His amazing leadership brought this home!"

Now Troy was lifted into the air, fake champagne spraying him from all around. From within the bubbly mist, his eyes met Chad's. They set Troy down next to their new star player.

"Speech, speech!" they demanded.

Troy gestured with one hand for them to settle down. Chad didn't notice, because from behind, Troy's free hand was gently caressing the small of the cheerleader's back. The blond's spine stiffened, but no one caught on. "I did a really stupid thing a while back," Troy said as Chad began to purr. "I quit the football team."

There were mock boos.

"I'll take that," he said, "especially because of why I left. I let my fears get in the way. I chose to play it safe. I went with a sport that was one man against another man. I didn't have to worry about letting anyone down. I didn't have to worry about anyone else letting me down. Today I got to be part of a team again. The fastest, strongest team this school has ever seen!"

The cries and locker-banging set Chad's ears to ringing, yet still he heard Troy loud and clear when he leaned back and whispered, "Follow me in five."

Amidst the hooting and hollering and back-clapping, Troy disappeared in the direction of the showers. Chad managed to wait sixty seconds before going after him. When he got there, all the nozzles were on full blast, filling the boys' shower room with hot steam and the sound of spattering water.

A form stepped forward, and there was Troy, dripping wet in his jockstrap. His chest was pumped and the veins stood out on his biceps, like he'd snuck in a few quick push-ups while he waited.

"Some game, huh?" he said, putting his hands behind his head. The pose made his skin pull tight over lean muscle.

"Yeah," the blond teen said, followed by an awkward cough. He was not quite sure where to look. "Shouldn't we..."

He gestured back to the guys, whose boisterous banter echoed their way.

"Definitely," Troy agreed, stepping forward. He gazed up and down at Chad, still in his football uniform. "I wish I could take a picture of you in all this gear."

"My dad got a couple of snaps," he laughed. "There's no way he's ever going to forget this day."

"For sure," Troy agreed, starting to lift Chad's No. 89 shirt over his head. "Let me help you with the straps." Troy's fingers lightly touched Chad's tan skin before undoing the binding holding his shoulder pads in place.

Chad's breathing quickened.

"Please don't tease me," he murmured, edging closer to Troy.

"No teasing," Troy said. "It's just, it would look weird for you to come into the shower room and leave dry."

"No fear of that," Chad whispered.

His shoulder pads dropped to the ground. He pushed down the football pants. His jock and cup clattered onto the floor as well.

"You wore underwear under your cup?" Troy smirked, gazing down at the tight red ginch Chad sported.

"Like I was going to put Riley's spare cup against my skin. No thank you."

Troy smiled, playing with the underwear's elastic band.

"They're hot," Troy said.

"I got them online," Chad stammered.

Troy took Chad's hand and pulled him into the mist. Troy's body pulsed with adrenalin. He was primed for taking risks. It took all Chad had not to hug him.

"Aren't you afraid?" Chad asked, jerking his chin towards the sound of blasting rock music. Someone had hooked an iPod up to speakers.

"Terrified," Troy admitted, a lump forming in his throat, and Chad regretted bringing it up.

"You did real good out there," Troy said, gazing at Chad's body.

He's going to chicken out, just like Jake, Chad realized, and the fear in his belly of being led on and then tossed aside was too much. He wrapped his arms around Troy's neck, and their lips pressed together. Troy held him tight, the jock's entire body trembling.

They pulled away by unspoken consent. They stood there, touching each other lightly, kissing, touching more, testing to make sure the other wasn't going to bolt. And just as they began to relax, to trust, to lower their guards, they both halted. Something was up. It took them several moments to realize what it was.

"The music's stopped," Troy said. They both stared in the direction of the locker room. The beats did not resume.

Troy stepped away, and the movement scooped out a piece of Chad's heart.

"Come on, Coach, we need our tunes," Markham was saying.

Troy and Chad appeared in the doorway, towels around their waists.

"Settle down," the coach yelled. It was then everyone noticed Principal McGee standing behind him.

"I have some very upsetting news," the coach began. "It's about Jesse."

"Jesse?" Troy whispered, his heart pounding harder.

"There's no easy way to say this," the coach continued, "but I want us to be together for this, to be there for each other, as a team." The coach took a deep breath, and Troy felt the tears build in his eyes.

"Please, no," he begged.

"Jesse's parents were out for the evening. When they came home they found him, in his room."

"This isn't happening," Troy insisted.

"He hanged himself."

There was something more after that, something about grief counselors, social workers trying to figure out why it happened, and there would be a memorial.

Troy heard none of it. He felt a hand on his shoulder.

It was Chad.

The hand pulled Troy in for a hug but Troy stepped back.

"I can't," he choked.

Everyone looked to Troy now, the whole team, to the man who'd led them to victory, and who was Jesse's best friend.

"I'm sorry, man," Adam said to him.

Troy ignored him, threw a zippy over his shoulders, got into a pair of track pants, yanked on his shoes, left all his gear in a heap, and took off.

"I should go after him," Chad said.

"No, son," his father said, holding him back. "Sometimes a man just needs to be alone with his grief."

Chapter 24

Liza gagged on the smell filling the Dedarling mansion. The bronze statue of Apollo in the foyer shared her revulsion. Devon's hands had been hard at work on it, shifting its serene face into a grimace. It looked more like a tormented spirit than the Greek god of art.

Liza took off her shoes to soften her steps as she walked up the staircase.

Down the hallway she went. It was dark. Some of the bulbs lining the wall in fanciful sconces still glowed—or tried to. They were wilted and misshapen, many of their filaments sputtering—more of Devon's handiwork.

She stopped before Mrs. Dedarling's studio, now the home of the Creation.

Devon was slouched in an armchair. A single lamp shone next to him.

The rank air was strongest here. Flies buzzed about excitedly.

"It died," Devon said, not looking up.

Raw-looking wounds clustered with flies wracked the Creation—what was left of it. Stubble raked its cheeks, and the cat litter around it was full of lumps.

"I'm sorry," Liza said.

"I couldn't do this on my own," he said. "We were supposed to be in this *together*."

"We are in this together," Liza insisted.

"So you're back?" he snorted. "Well, maybe I don't want you anymore."

"Please," she begged, running to his side, getting to her knees and clutching his pant legs. "I made a mistake. I thought..."

"That they'd be there for you? They let you down, didn't they?"

"Yes." It came out barely a whisper.

"Just like you let me down."

"I can make things right," she said enthusiastically, her head bobbing and her face smiling. "Remember how good things were? How happy we were before..."

"Before you dumped me?" Devon said with a surly tone.

"Yes," she agreed, her grip on his pant leg loosening, and her smile withering. She seemed to shrink, and looked to the exit. The thought of her leaving made Devon rustle uncomfortably.

"How can I trust you now?" he asked defensively.

"I brought you something."

She took him by the hand—he noted the way she clasped it. He could destroy her right here, right now, twist her beyond recognition. She met his gaze. She knew it too. She gripped tighter, and pulled him up from his chair. He followed her into the hall, down the stairs, and into the front foyer.

Standing there, in a trance, was Evan, still in his football uniform. The statue of Apollo's face seemed to howl in futile warning.

"For you," Liza said as Devon circled the jock like a shark.

Devon stopped, stroking the stud's strong jaw.

"No," he said, "not for me."

"Please," Liza begged, not even trying to hide her desperation now. "I don't belong in that world. I belong here, with you."

Devon held up a finger for silence.

"I said, not for *me*," he repeated, "but for *us*."

He held his hand out to her and pulled her close. They kissed long and hard. She waited for him to feel her body the way Evan did, but Devon did not.

It's okay, she assured herself, *I can live without that.*

He kept an arm around her as he turned his attention back to the football player, and slowly sank his fingers into his chest.

Chapter 25

Dear Diary,

I can't take it. Everything is so messed up. It's like the world is melt-ing. I DON'T KNOW WHAT TO DO OR HOW TO MAKE SENSE OF IT!

"Suicide Tragedy Strikes Nuffim High Football Team" was the paper's front-page headline the next morning. Troy turned it face down as he drank his protein shake in the Allstars' cheery yellow kitchen. His dad watched him with worry.

Their doorbell rang. It was the coach.

"I'm picking up everyone from the team," he explained.

"You don't have to go to school today," Troy's dad started, but the jock had already grabbed his bag and was following the coach out.

"Son!" Troy's dad grabbed him. "It's okay to cry. You know that, right?"

"Sure," Troy said, his face stony and without expression.

"If you can't talk about it, you can always write about it," his dad added. "Make a list if you want, of your feelings, whatever... and it *is* okay to cry."

Troy recalled his dad's words during the silent drive to school.

When they got to Nuffim High, his teammates headed for their homerooms, but the coach held Troy back. "There's someone in my office who wants to talk to you." Troy followed numbly. He didn't even react when he saw the two police officers waiting for him in the coach's office. They sat him down.

"You were Jesse's best friend," the officer on the right said.

"Yes," Troy replied.

"Well then," the officer on the left continued, "maybe you could explain this."

He flipped open a laptop and clicked play on a media window. The image was grainy and there was no sound, lending it a surreal quality, but it was clearly a video of Jesse in the school locker room, kissing Troy's bare torso.

There was a snap—the sound of the laptop popping shut—and only then did Troy realize the video was over. Everyone stared at him.

Troy felt like he floated, not touched by any of it.

"This video," the officer on the right said, "was emailed to your best friend yesterday. By the end of the day, we had a dead teenager on our hands."

Troy waited. This was it. The officer put his hand on Troy's shoulder.

"We need you to come clean."

Troy opened his mouth, ready to tell them everything.

"Do you know who the other person in the video is?" the officer continued.

Troy blinked.

"You...you don't know?"

"We can only make out Jesse's face," the first cop said. "Did Jesse tell you anything? Mention anyone?"

Troy hesitated.

"No. No one special."

The cops looked to each other in disappointment.

"Do you have any idea who might have sent this?"

Troy's face grew hard.

Mandy.

"No," he lied once more.

The officers' frustration and skepticism were clear. They kept jabbing Troy in the gut. He felt nauseous. He flexed the discomfort out. All he had to do was stay stony and hard. Just let everything bounce off.

"Okay, but if there's someone you're protecting..."

"There isn't," Troy insisted.

Only me.

The police packed up and left, leaving Troy alone with the coach. The big man came and sat next to him, worry in his eyes.

"I didn't want to say anything in front of the cops, but...it wasn't Chad, was it?"

"Chad?"

"In the video, with Jesse. He didn't..."

"Do you really think he's the only faggot in school?" Troy snapped.

The coach pulled back. For just a moment, something had rippled across the serene waters holding Troy warm and safe. Troy hunched down in his chair. No textbook posture for him today. There was light stubble on his unshaven cheeks. His shirt and pants were rumpled.

"Don't say it like that," the coach chided.

"The guys in the locker room talk like that all the time."

Another ripple.

Anger, he thought to himself, *I'm feeling angry.* It was as if he were a jeweler appraising a gem he'd heard of but never truly taken the time to examine.

"Well, yeah," the coach agreed, "but as an insult."

"Well maybe that's the problem" Troy muttered.

"What?"

"Nothing. Look, it wasn't Chad, okay?"

The coach nodded.

"Okay."

Troy grabbed his bag.

It was me.

Mandy searched through her locker. She was certain she kept a bottle of Chanel here, *quite* certain in fact, but it was gone.

"Chad, did you take my perfume?" she asked.

He stood two lockers over.

"No," he replied.

"It's okay if you did," Mandy said. "I just need it back."

"I've switched to Gaultier," he replied.

"Wow, you win one football game and now you're all butch."

"Have you been in my locker?" he asked Mandy.

"Probably," she shrugged.

"Did you take anything?"

"Nothing worth taking," she replied.

"Oh, I guess I left it at home," he said to himself, closing his locker.

"Mandy, I need to talk with you."

It was Troy who spoke.

"Troy," she said, sadness in her voice. She wrapped her arms around him.

"I'm so sorry."

He didn't hug back.

"Hi, Troy," Chad added, hoping for a similar embrace.

Troy didn't even look at him. He grabbed Mandy's wrists and roughly pulled her off of him.

"Hey," she said.

His fingers dug into her.

"You're hurting me."

"Good."

Her force field popped on and broke his grip.

"Just because Jesse died doesn't mean..."

"He saw the video," Troy said.

"What are you talking about?" Mandy asked.

"You know exactly what I'm talking about. The one you took. Of Jesse, and me, in the locker room." He said the last bit in a hushed whisper that Chad's hearing had no problem picking up.

"I deleted that," Mandy hissed.

"Then why were two cops showing it to me just now in the coach's office? Someone sent that video to Jesse the day he killed himself."

"Oh God," Mandy breathed, "I didn't, Troy. I swear. I erased it. I didn't show it to anyone, not even Chad. You have to believe me. You can sense it, right?"

"Actually, I can't," he said, keeping his insides hard as granite. If he let go, let anything in, reached out, he knew he'd shatter. His gut tightened at the thought.

"Please," Mandy sobbed, "I would never try to hurt anyone like that."

"Just go," he said.

"Come on," Chad said, taking her by the shoulders.

He led her away, only once looking back.

Troy didn't bother watching them leave. He punched his locker, but instead of a satisfying metallic bang there was a muffled squelch. He pulled his fist back and stringy bits of clay-like material stuck to his knuckles. The strands looked to be melted bits of the locker door. He wiped it off, puzzled but not prepared to take on this mystery right now.

Instead, he opened his lock and stared at his neatly arranged shelves of textbooks. His eyes scanned for the one thing that could help him keep his grip right now—just a little something to take off the edge. He didn't see it. He moved books aside. His search grew frantic, but though he yanked out binders, and even his lucky football, it was no use.

What he sought was not to be found.

He banged his head against the locker next to his. He didn't dare free a tear. If he did, he knew his shredded insides, which he was barely holding together, would forever fall apart.

The morning started very differently for Devon and Liza.

She hummed a tune that made Devon smile. He wore a decadent white bathrobe that Mrs. Dedarling had swiped from a boutique hotel in Dubai. He sat on a stool at the island in the middle of the kitchen, reading the headlines with satisfaction. There was a hiss from Liza's direction as she poured homemade batter into a stainless steel waffle iron. Bacon and eggs sizzled in separate pans on the six-burner stove. Her hair was freshly washed and she smelled of lavender and rosemary.

Mrs. Dedarling had been a big fan of Aveeda shampoo.

With a bubbling joy Liza served up the eggs, bacon, and waffles. The toaster popped the freshly baked bread she'd picked up. The two teens sat side by side, eating the small feast. With the Creation dead there was actually time for normal domestic bliss. A bit, anyway. Liza snagged the comics section and when she giggled, Devon actually paid attention, leaning over with a smile.

"What's so funny?" he asked.

"Oh, just *Ziggy*," she said.

"I like *The Far Side*," he said with a smile, giving her a kiss on the forehead.

"That felt nice," Liza said, snapping the end off her bacon with her teeth.

He nudged her shoulder with his, making her giggle some more. She kept eating, he kept reading, and her eyes wandered around the kitchen.

"How are we going to keep paying for this place?"

"Don't ruin it," Devon chided.

"What?"

"I'm happy, you're happy, let's just enjoy the moment."

"I am," she insisted. "I'm just saying the future..."

"...will happen with or without us worrying about the mortgage," Devon cut in.

"Okay, hon. I'm just glad that I don't have to hang out with Mandy anymore."

"Well," Devon corrected, "at least only for a bit longer."

She set down the syrup.

"I thought things were going to be different."

"They are," Devon said.

"So why do I have to still pretend to be her friend, especially after last night?"

"Here's why."

He pulled up his knapsack and dumped the contents on the counter. She picked up *Star Trek* trading cards, a bottle of Chanel, a plastic prescription bottle with some anti-anxiety pills in it, and a bright pink Barbie journal.

"I grabbed a few things from your friends' lockers."

"They're not my friends," she said.

"Soon, they won't be anything"—he pointed to the journal—"thanks to that."

"*Dear Diary*," she read from the tome of Barbie, "*You had totally better be sitting down for this because you are NOT going to believe what happened after school today.*"

"Come on," he said. "You can read that later. It's the shiz, but we don't want to be late for school."

She followed him out into the foyer. He was already putting his backpack on.

"You're going to school today?" she asked.

He stared at what was left of Evan Mueller. He was stripped down to his football pants, his form melded to the statue of Apollo.

"Liza, please," the football jock rasped, though it came out a mumbled jumble, his lips partially fused with Apollo's.

Liza regarded him coldly. "You should've loved me when you had the chance. Now it's too late. For all of you."

"Darling," Devon said to Liza, "we have to get going. It's time to take our art out into the world."

Chapter 26

Devon and Liza had to run the gauntlet of journalists, photographers, and TV cameras piled in front of the school to get through the front doors that morning.

"This is awesome," he said to her.

"Sign-up sheets for grief counseling are over there!" the principal shouted.

"Yeah right," Devon said, taking Liza's hand and giving it a squeeze. She blushed like a virgin bride.

"Like there's such a shortage of jocks," she said, pleased with his wink of approval. Her feelings for Evan were already a hazy memory in her mind, as if he were a painting and her brain had dumped turpentine all over it. Nor had he been reported missing. Liza had phoned his mom that morning, imitating his voice perfectly, explaining how he'd crashed at a bud's after the game. And today at school, everyone was too busy with Jesse's death to be bothered with a missing football player, who was probably at home grieving. Still, Devon didn't want to be too obvious, and he pulled his hand away from Liza's.

"Don't want to give us away," he said.

She nodded in reluctant agreement. His touch was still warm

on her palm.

This was real, not the fantasy she'd tried to engage in with a football dud. For a moment the blurry portrait of her boyfriend melded with Apollo grew sharp.

He would've left me, she assured herself, *if not for someone taller*—he was an unashamed height-hunter—*then for someone prettier. And he would've expected me to be grateful that he'd given me any time at all. With Devon, I have a future.*

The PA announcements that morning were all about "do not speak with the journalists outside unless you are comfortable doing so" and "group counseling will be available during lunch hour, and individual counseling throughout the day," and, of course, "please support the bake sale. Proceeds will go towards the Jesse Truesden memorial."

"Liza?" Mandy asked from her seat behind the tall girl.

"Yes?" Liza replied hesitantly, detecting a note of suspicion.

"When I drove you home, and you sang me to sleep, how long was I out for?"

"Like half-a-second," Liza replied, and then, with a nervous laugh, "Relax, you didn't snore."

Mandy nodded doubtfully, still wondering how that video got sent to Jesse. On a day when everyone else wore black, Liza's color of choice was a bright pink shawl over a tight baby blue shirt that showed off her cleavage. There was a bit of glitter next to each eye.

The final announcement distracted Mandy. "A commemoration assembly will be held tomorrow morning."

Devon slipped Liza a note. She read his scrawled handwriting. *"The assembly."*

It said no more because there was nothing more that needed to be said. Liza looked at her classmates—soon to be her former classmates—and slipped the note between her breasts, just as she'd once done with Evan's number. The memorial truly would be memorable, for anyone who survived it.

When the bell rang, Mandy waited while Liza got up.

"Oh, you go ahead, girl," Liza shooed. "I'm going to...go for one of those grief counseling thingies."

"Sure," Mandy said. "Okay."

It was a busy day for Liza. Art required fresh material, and not just anyone would do. They were done with online losers and would-be football stars.

"Hey Chad," she said, walking up to the blond teen as the final bell rang, "I want to show you something."

"Okay," he said trustingly.

He followed her out to the parking lot, stopping next to her aunt's rusty pickup truck. The whole time he was thinking about Troy, about the video sent to Jesse, trying to figure out who could've done it.

If I can find the person responsible, maybe Troy will like me again.

He pictured Troy's look of gratitude, his strong arms hugging Chad tight, Troy saying, "You're my queero."

And that's when Chad noticed Liza's scent.

"Are you wearing Chanel?" he asked.

The perfume wasn't enough to hide her smell of nervousness. Liza began to sing and the lullaby made him sway drunkenly.

"What're you..."

Devon got out of Liza's aunt's pickup. None of this was adding up. Only it finally was. Whether it was animal instinct or a simple leap of logic, Chad figured it out.

"It was you who sent Jesse that video," he said, his voice starting to slur.

"Help me get him in the truck," Devon ordered.

Chad did not make it home that day.

Chapter 27

There was a certain justice to the next stage of Devon's plan happening in the cafeteria, at least in Liza's mind. The following morning she sat at the table that the group she infiltrated had co-opted, if only briefly, uniting a jock, a nerd, a loner and a couple of cheerleaders as even *The Breakfast Club* could not.

Gibbie sat with her. He wore a dark suit that looked two sizes too big, accentuating his skinny frame.

"Forget it," he finally said, getting up to go.

Liza grabbed him. "Wait!"

"I hate Chad. I don't even know how he talked me into this."

"But do you hate him, Gibbie, or are your feelings hurt because you actually really like him?" Liza countered.

Gibbie hesitated. The truth was every time the phone rang, he hoped it was Chad calling. Last night he finally got what he wanted, and almost demanded to know what had taken the male cheerleader so long.

And then Chad said the words Gibbie had been dying to hear.

"I made a mistake."

So then why is Liza here, he wondered, *and how do I get rid of her so Chad and I can be alone?*

"Here," she said, "have some of my juice."

He drank it thirstily—he was rather parched after the salty crackers Liza had been feeding him to help appease his nervous stomach. He finished it off as Mandy stopped before them, slamming a Gucci bag onto the table. Her skintight black dress clung to her arms and ended just below her ass. Her round black hat had a gauzy veil over her eyes. She pulled out a compact to touch up her lips.

"No offense, guys," she said, "but Chad's meeting me here this morning for a super important talk before the memorial, so I need the table. Vamoose."

She snapped the compact shut and made shooing motions with her hands.

"What?" Gibbie demanded. "Chad called and said he wanted to talk with *me*."

Mandy glared at Liza.

"I suppose he called you too?"

"Not exactly," she smirked, thinking about how fun it had been to imitate Chad's voice on his cellphone, leading the pair on. "He has something he needs to tell you two, but he was too embarrassed. So he asked me to give you both this."

She handed them the Barbie diary, open to a very specific page.

Gibbie and Mandy read quickly, eyes roving over words with the I's dotted with hearts, and T's crossed with happy faces. When they'd finished reading Gibbie closed it, a dark look on his face.

"He really wants to talk with you guys about this," Liza said.

"Really?" Mandy asked tartly. "And where might we find him?"

"Where else?" Liza smirked. "Girls' locker room."

"I have to find Troy," Gibbie seethed, still clutching the journal.

Liza nodded. "I can see why you'd be pissed at him." She nodded towards the diary. "I mean, Chad's a slut, but your own brother?"

Gibbie's face was turning deep red. She stared at the empty bottle of juice and smiled. There was a bit of residue from the amphetamines she'd dissolved in it. Hopefully he had a strong heart. He got up, ready to storm off.

"Wait!" Liza cried.

Her cellphone beeped and she quickly read a text message. Looking back at Gibbie, she said, "Try the weight room."

Mandy and Liza walked briskly through the school's near-deserted halls. Students had been told to go directly to the auditorium. Liza struggled to keep up with Mandy's clip-clapping high-heeled tread.

In a pitch that only animals could hear, Liza began to sing. A loud banging suddenly rose up from the girls' change room.

"Chad?" Mandy called, hurrying towards it. Behind her Liza sang harder. Outside, dogs yelped in pain. The banging grew more frenzied.

Mandy pushed open the door and clattered her way towards a metal supply cabinet next to a poster of the human anatomy. The cabinet rattled wildly, as if trying to contain a rabid elephant. The doors bulged with bumps from being punched from the inside.

Mandy reached for the release handle...

Do it, Liza gloated.

...and the cheerleader spun around and grabbed Liza by the collar. Mandy was surprisingly strong, and in a new twist on the peer cheer, she rammed Liza against a row of lockers.

"I know when I'm being played," Mandy seethed.

This was not part of the plan. Liza had lulled Chad to sleep, locked him in the cabinet this morning until Mandy came to meet him, and then Liza woke him with her voice, using it to drive him into a frenzy in a frequency beyond Mandy's hearing. Liza didn't want Mandy crazed. She wanted the head cheerleader to be aware that her best friend was ripping her apart. The end, or so Liza had hoped.

No matter. On to Plan B. Liza began to sing a soothing lullaby. "Hush, little baby, don't say a word..."

Mandy head butted her with her force field. There was a loud crack, Liza screamed in pain, and rivulets of dark blood ran down from her nose.

"Did you really think I didn't know about Chad macking with my ex-boyfriend?" Mandy demanded. "It was you who sent that video to Jesse."

Any answer was cut off by the sound of ripping metal. Chad's clawed fist broke through the cabinet door, scratching wildly at the empty air. Mandy didn't flinch. She turned on Liza.

"You try to use your voice on me again and I'll crack your skull, understand?"

Liza nodded.

"Now what have you done to Chad?"

Liza opened her mouth to answer, but no sound that Mandy could hear came out. Dogs outside yelped in pain. Chad's growl grew to a full-on howl and the rattle of metal was like thunder. Mandy drew her head back, ready to smash her force field into Liza's forehead, but the doors of the utility closet burst open and Chad crashed out, toppling into Mandy and knocking her away from Liza.

They went down in a spree of flailing limbs and tearing claws. Mandy caught flashes of silver from the skimpy Speedo Devon had dressed the blond in. Otherwise Chad was unclothed.

He slashed and bit at her. His fangs broke and his claws cracked on her force field. Blood frothed from his gums. His skin glistened with baby oil.

"Stop it!" Mandy shouted. "You're hurting yourself."

Her force field crackled around her.

He just bit all the harder, the pain sending him into a greater frenzy.

"Leave him alone!" Mandy yelled at Liza. "You're killing him."

"No," Liza smiled grimly, pulling out a video camera. "You're killing him. This is so *Saw*. Do you keep your force field up to protect yourself while your friend breaks himself against it, or do you lower it, and let your friend rip you apart? Tough call. Ready for your close-up?"

The red light on the camera blinked as Liza released another high-pitched wail and Chad's claws drew back, aiming for Mandy's throat.

Troy watched veins snake across his arms as he pumped out a set of curls in the school's weight room. He was shirtless, dressed only in short shorts, socks, and sneakers. Behind Troy, his suit was hanging from a hook on the wall. He'd jogged here with it over one shoulder, protected by a garbage bag.

People would start arriving for the assembly soon, Troy would make a speech, and yet all the same, here he was, letting off some steam—or trying to raise it.

Truth was, Troy felt no steam to let off. He was back to where he was before he'd drunk that bottle of Etienne water. Emotions, including his own, were like foreign invaders for his immune system to subdue. At least the weights gave him muscular pain.

He changed into his suit, buttoning up his shirt, not even bothering to shower. The door banged open, and in stomped Gibbie.

"We need to talk," he said.

"Walk with me," Troy replied, doing up his tie and heading towards the door.

Gibbie grabbed him by the arm.

"Are you okay?" Troy asked. "Your pupils are really dilated."

"We need to talk *now*," Gibbie shouted, and with a jerk of the arm he sent Troy flying across the room.

Chapter 28

Mandy screamed, jerking and twisting her body in a desperate attempt to dislodge Chad. Liza gazed at her watch.

"Good work, Mandy, you've held your shield up for five minutes now. That's 30 seconds longer than your record. Must be the desperation. Still, adrenalin can only take you so far."

With a final jolt that sent Chad hopping back in surprise, Mandy's shield pulsed briefly, and then fizzled into nothing.

"What do you know," Liza tittered.

Chad growled, muscular arms clenched on either side of him, sweat staining his little silver Speedo. He pounced.

Mandy vanished from sight. He landed on concrete. There was a scratch of movement and he reared about, leaping at apparent nothingness.

Mandy flashed into visibility and fell backwards under his weight. He tumbled over her, rolling in a somersault that landed him squarely on his feet a few paces from his best friend, who he was attempting to kill. Mandy tried to get up; the heel of her shoe snapped and she fell, banging her elbow hard on the concrete floor. Chad hissed and pounced again. Mandy knew it was futile to try scrambling out of the way. Even if she stood up quickly enough, he'd simply tear into her calves a second later.

There was no point in disappearing. He could smell and hear her. And her shield was tapped out. It was time to perform. She drew on all her years of competing at cheerleader championships. Her insides grew calm and steady. She pressed her shoulder blades, palms, and the bottom of her ass into the floor. She felt anchored.

Lay-down position.

Chad came barreling towards her.

She kicked off her shoes. She didn't want to puncture him with her heels.

He flew through the air, about to land right on top of her. His claws extended towards her throat. Her legs reared up, knees bent. His stomach rammed into the bottoms of her feet. She grunted as his mass bore into her.

Leg tuck, she chanted to herself, reducing this life-and-death situation to the most banal of cheerleading moves.

In one fluid movement she clenched and jerked her legs back and over her head, taking Chad's momentum and sending him flying—directly at Liza.

"Holy fu—," Liza cursed.

She took a deep breath, but before she could let out a vibratory blast, he rammed into her, the claws on his toes digging deep into her sides. She screamed now, in unfocused pain, and the entire room shook.

She turned her voice on Chad, blasting him off her in a wave of sound. He tore strips out of her as he was whipped into a set of lockers. He lay there panting and dazed.

"Get ready for your ears to bleed," Liza growled, her brow dripping with sweat.

"I don't think so," Mandy replied.

Liza turned with a start and Mandy sucker-punched her across the jaw. Liza staggered backward and Mandy grimaced at the pain in her wrist, shaking her hand in the air.

"You are so dead," Liza cursed. She inhaled and let go a blaring scream. Mandy snapped into invisibility and got out of the way barely in time. The wall where she'd stood exploded into the neighboring room.

Mandy tried to hold her invisibility, but she banged into a fallen bench. She warbled back into view. Liza took another deep breath. Mandy's shield sparked and then fizzled into nothing. She was out of juice.

"I thought we were friends," Mandy panted.

"I could never be friends with the likes of you," Liza said with disgust.

Mandy hugged herself for protection, squeezing her eyes shut, preparing for her own demise.

"That's right, cow," Liza smiled. "This is for a lifetime of humiliation."

There was a sharp intake of breath.

Mandy flinched, waiting for the end.

Seconds passed. Then seconds more.

Mandy opened her eyes.

Chad stood behind Liza. One of his fingers was pressed deep into the side of the girl's throat. He panted heavily and made a quick jerky motion with the embedded digit. Liza gasped. Chad yanked his finger out of her, leaving a bloody hole in her neck.

Liza dropped to her knees, gripping the wound.

Rivulets of red seeped through her fingers.

"What is the matter with you?" Troy demanded of his little brother, struggling to get back on his feet.

Gibbie grabbed the jock by the throat and pressed him against the wall.

"You made out with him," Gibbie said, his grip tightening.

"Yes," Troy said, squirming in an attempt to wriggle free. "I kissed Jesse. I should've told you I'm gay. I just couldn't..."

Gibbie flung him aside.

"Chad!" the younger boy yelled. "You made out with Chad!"

His rage pounded over Troy like fists.

Beat it down, Troy told himself, *shut it in the room.*

He forced the feelings behind a door in his mind, which began to bulge with the strain. Gibbie picked up an eighty-pound barbell in one hand, holding it like a javelin.

"I can explain," Troy panted.

The barbell crashed into the wall next to Troy's head.

"You can explain?" Gibbie demanded. "You can explain why you stuck your tongue down the throat of a guy you barely noticed before? A guy you knew I worshipped? The guy I've wanted to be with since *before* I got pubic hair?"

"You have pubic hair?" Troy asked, genuinely surprised.

A second barbell smashed near his head.

Gibbie looked about for more things to throw. His eyes alighted upon stacks of weighted plates.

"This isn't you," Troy panted. "I know you, Gibbie. No matter how mad you got, you'd never try to kill me."

Gibbie flung a forty-five-pound plate like a discus. Troy dove out of the way and it smashed into the wall, sticking there and vibrating.

Gibbie's eyes were completely bloodshot at this point.

"You're drugged," Troy said.

Gibbie gripped the weightlifting machine in the middle of the room—a squarish affair of rusting metal with stations around it for squats, bench presses, shoulder raises, and bicep curls, all attached to stacks of weights by pulleys and cables. Gibbie pushed the entire machine towards his brother. It was too big to get around, bearing down on the jock like a Mack truck.

"Oh shiii—"

It slammed into him, and pushed him towards the wall, ready to crush him. Troy squirmed and managed to wedge himself between the equipment's vertical bars just in time to avoid being caught between them and the cinder-block wall. They smashed together, and there was a whining of metal as the machine began to crumple under Gibbie's strength.

Troy found himself unhurt, but barred in by what was left of the machine.

Gibbie reached for his brother, and grunted in frustration at not being able to grab him. Troy was caged in, but Gibbie was caged out.

Gibbie stalked to the opposite side of the machine and began pressing against it, squashing it slowly as if it were in a trash compactor. The bars began bending in towards Troy.

"Listen to me!" Troy yelled, trying to reach out with feelings of calm and reason. They slithered off Gibbie like skin from a molting snake.

"You're amped on speed or something," Troy said.

The machine crunched against his leg.

"You're hurting me!" he screamed.

There was another crunch and his arm was pinned.

A piece of jagged metal pressed against his chest, on target for his heart.

Gibbie took a moment to catch his breath.

"So why'd you do it, Troy? I want to hear you say it."

"Gibbie, I never meant to..."

Gibbie leaned into the machine.

"You did it to screw me over! I was finally stronger than you, so you took the one thing I really wanted."

The metal shaft ripped Troy's shirt and broke his skin. Warm blood trickled down his chest.

"I love him!" Troy shouted.

The machine stopped.

The silence after the bedlam was deafening.

"You *what?*" Gibbie demanded.

"I love him," Troy repeated.

To his own wonder, he meant it, and saying it opened the door—not in his head, but in his heart, and it felt warm.

I'm going to die. My brother's going to kill me.

Yet still he felt a moment of peace.

"What do you love about him?" Gibbie demanded suspiciously.

His body, Troy thought. But it was more than that.

There were momentary flashes of Chad, cheerleading, triple-snapping during lunch hour, being sent to the principal's office for showing up in a *Legally Blonde* T-shirt cut off at the midriff.

"He's not afraid to be himself," Troy said.

There was another pause.

"Gibbie?"

"Yeah?"

"I love you too."

Saying the words once again pulled up memories, of pouting at the hospital while his mom showed him his new baby brother, and then years later, the two of them wearing matching head-to-ankle snowsuits while tobogganing together, and, more recently, jumping off the docks at their grandparents' cottage, seeing who could make the biggest splash. The waves of attachment flowed from Troy to Gibbie, stronger and deeper than any drug.

"Troy?"

"Yeah, Gibbie?"

"I love you too."

There was a squeal of metal on concrete as Gibbie pulled the weight machine back. Troy gasped as the pressure on his leg and arm fell away and blood flowed back into them.

Gibbie walked around, looking a little bashful.

"So do you *really* love him?"

"I do."

Gibbie's shoulders slumped.

"I really messed up, huh?" Troy asked.

He wrapped his arm around his little brother.

"Chad was never going to go for me anyway," Gibbie sighed.

Troy felt the slap of defeat wash off his brother. Gibbie wiped at his eyes.

"I just get tired of being a loser, you know?"

"You're not a loser," Troy said. "You're tough. To take what you take, every day, to find joy in your world of make-believe—that takes a lot of strength."

"Things were a lot clearer when I was just pretending to have power," Gibbie replied.

"No rolling the dice in the real world, huh? Come on," Troy said, hugging Gibbie. "Let's get to the assembly."

"You're not mad at me?" Gibbie pressed.

Troy looked down at his torn shirt and rumpled suit.

"I'll get over it. You're not mad at me?"

"Really pissed," Gibbie conceded. "But I guess I might as well get used to the fact that you're the kind of guy who gets everything, and I'm not."

"My life's not that simple," Troy said. "Jesse and I...we...we were more than friends, and now..."

Troy waited for the tears, but still they wouldn't come.

Gibbie wrapped his arms around his older brother and hugged him tight.

"Come on," Gibbie said, "you've got a speech to make."

They got up and made it as far as the door, when Troy stopped.

"How did you know I made out with Chad?"

Gibbie pulled out the Barbie journal, open to the incriminating page.

Troy took it.

"Where did you get this?"

Before Gibbie could answer, the wall behind them began to vibrate, and then blew in, spraying concrete blocks everywhere.

Chapter 29

Chad's shoulders heaved up and down, his rib cage expanding and contracting with ragged breaths. He stared down at Liza, lying on the floor. Blood formed in a pool about her. With a gentle sigh his claws retracted and with a shake of his head his pointed ears became normal.

"Chad?" Mandy asked uncertainly.

He opened his eyes. They were a piercing blue. He gazed at a poster of the human anatomy taped to a whiteboard, then over to the cabinet doors he'd shredded. Beyond that was the hole Liza had blown through the wall. Shattered cement blocks littered the floor.

"I'm okay," he said. "She got me real revved up, but I'm okay."

Mandy stood next to him and curled her fingers into the crook of his shapely arm. She looked down at Liza. The large girl made a gurgling sound.

"She's not dead," Mandy said with wonder.

"No," Chad said, "she's not. I avoided the arteries."

Liza's eyes fluttered open. Chad went over to the cabinet he'd been locked in and yanked out the first aid kit. He pulled free a roll of gauze, and began wrapping it around Liza's neck. She looked up at him in wonder.

"I suppose you're wondering why I'm helping you after you tried to kill us."

She gazed at him mutely. Chad extended one of his nails and Liza flinched. He used it to cut the gauze and then he taped it in place. There was already a circle of blood coming through.

"My dad used to introduce me to his buddies as his Little Animal, and make a *grrr* noise," said Chad. "He hasn't called me that in a long time, not since he caught me putting my G.I. Joes in dresses. Screw him, I figured. But he was right, you know. I am an animal—and not just a peacock. It's always been in me. It's wild, and predatory, and hungry. It's also very precise."

He looked up at the anatomy poster and then back to her.

"I cut your vocal cords, Liza. You won't hurt anybody else with your voice."

Tears bubbled in her eyes.

"I know what you're thinking," Chad said. "You wish I had killed you instead. But unlike you, Liza, I'm not a killer. I'm sorry you got teased all these years. I'm sorry for the teasing that I did. But as a fag whose father hates him, I know that we all have choices. You can suck it up. You can shut it down. You can take revenge. Or you can be so goddamn fabulous that you change the world, and make it your own. You had a choice, Liza. Jesse had a choice. To make the world a better place."

There was a tear in Liza's eye. She mouthed the words, "*I hate you.*"

"Sometimes I hate me too," Chad agreed. "Doesn't make murder cool, though. And another thing—if you ever come for me or any of my friends ever again, I still won't kill you. But I will cut your tongue off. If that doesn't convince you to leave us alone, your fingers will be next. Do you understand?"

She nodded.

"Good girl."

Mandy gazed at him with wonder, and a touch of fear.

"Damn. You really are fierce."

Before he could answer, they both heard a buzzing from Liza's purse. It was her cellphone vibrating. Mandy pulled it out.

"Devon sent her a text message," she said, staring at the call display.

Chad's fake-and-bake tan went ashen.

"What?" she asked. "You look like you're going to hurl, and not in an 'I want to stay thin' kind of way."

"What does it say?" he asked.

Mandy flipped open the phone, and read, "Where are you? It's time."

They looked at each other with worried expressions.

"Too bad she can't talk anymore," Mandy said, jerking her head towards Liza.

Chad kneeled down and picked up a pair of paper scraps that had fallen out of Liza's purse.

"She doesn't have to."

He handed them to Mandy.

"*The Assembly*," she read, and then the other one: "*Hit List: Nuffim High*."

They stood staring at each other.

"Well," Mandy said, "since the fat lady's finished singing, I guess it's over."

"No," Chad said. "Devon's like us. He's got the power to...twist things."

"The whole assembly?" Mandy pressed.

Chad nodded. "They showed me their 'Creation.' It was all these people, what was left of them, melded together. Give me her phone."

He took it from Mandy's outstretched hand and hit No. 1 on Liza's speed-dial. Devon's name popped up as it started to ring.

"Where the hell are you?" Devon snapped from the other end.

"There's been a change in plans," Chad replied calmly.

Stunned silence greeted him.

"Your girlfriend's lying in a pool of her own blood," Chad continued. "She's still alive but she needs help."

"I'm going to kill you!" Devon yelled.

"Game on," Chad replied, snapping the phone shut.

"Fierce," Mandy smiled, holding her hand up for a high-five.

Their palms slapped together.

"We should warn Troy and Gibbie," Mandy said.

"Warn us about what?" Troy asked.

The two cheerleaders turned around and looked at the Allstar brothers, both of them roughed up in their suits. They stood on the other side of the hole Liza had blown through the wall. They stared down at her.

"We were set up," Mandy said to Gibbie.

"I was starting to think that," he replied.

"We've still got Devon to deal with," Chad piped in.

"From our class?" Troy asked.

"Apparently he's planning to pull a Carrie at the assembly," Mandy said, and then, to Chad, "You know, you kind of blew the whole element of surprise thing by calling him like that."

"Like I said, we all have a choice," Chad said. "I didn't want to take that away from him. He can come help Liza, or go ahead with his plan. Besides, you can turn invisible. How much more of an element of surprise do we need?"

"When did you get so smart?" she asked.

"I prefer the word *conniving*. And it was last year, when I seduced the captain of the football team."

"You seduced Jake Saunders?" Troy demanded.

"And how," Chad triple-snapped.

"Don't forget this year's captain of the wrestling team,"

Mandy added.

"Does *everybody* know?" Troy demanded.

"Is that a problem?" Chad asked.

"No," Gibbie said, looking at Chad, "it's not a problem."

In return Chad mouthed the words "*thank you.*"

"So, what's the plan for stopping psycho boy?" Gibbie asked.

"Wait for him to come to us. Four against one," Chad shrugged. Gazing at himself in the mirror, he twisted to see his ass in the silver Speedo. "Wow, they really had a nerd-on for Flash Gordon, and I am *totally* carrying it off."

"Uh, yeah," Troy cut in, "unless Devon *doesn't* come for her, in which case he takes out 99 per cent of the student body."

"Oh," Chad replied, "I guess I just figured true love would prevail."

"Here's what we do," Troy continued. "Mandy and Gibbie, you guys stay here in case he comes for Liza. Chad, you're with me. You've got his scent. Let's track him down, and maybe with a little empathic push I can convince him not to go Columbine on our butts. Cool?"

He looked to Gibbie.

"Yeah," Gibbie said, "it's cool."

Chad pushed on the door to get out. It didn't budge.

"Uh, guys, I think we might be locked in."

"Let me try," Troy said with exasperation. "It's probably just stuck."

The horizontal handle rattled in his grip but the door wouldn't move.

"Gibbie," Troy called.

There was a crack and a dull thump echoed in the room. Troy turned and saw Gibbie on the floor, unconscious, a trickle of blood running from his skull. For an instant it filled Troy with fury—except that the sight of the attacker made him go completely numb.

It was Jesse. The dead teen stood there, leering at them all, a dumbbell in his hand, red with Gibbie's blood. The dead youth was dressed only in football pants. His lips cracked a demented smile.

"Let's get this party started."

Chapter 30

"Jesse!" Troy said, about to rush towards his friend.

Chad grabbed the elder Allstar brother by the arm.

"That's not Jesse," Chad said, "not the way you knew him anyway. Devon's scent is all over him."

"Devon?" Troy asked, his eyes narrowing. Even with his empathy muted, he still felt anger coming from within his buddy's body, but not from him. It was almost as if someone else inhabited Jesse's form. Mandy was closest to Jesse and took a swing at him. He caught her hand, force field and all.

"Nice pants," she said, referring to his football bottoms. "Too bad you forgot your helmet."

She head-butted him with her shield crackling away, but instead of the expected *ka-thud* sound, there was a muffled *phu-losh*, and her shield sank into his face as if it were soft butter. She pulled away, and strings of Jesse's gooey flesh came with her.

"Time to free the statue within," he said. He pressed his whole body against her, hugging her as tight as he could. The field protected her but his skin began to crawl onto it, not trying to penetrate it, but sluicing all over the surface. His muscles globbed onto the barrier, the flesh flinging itself around her field like a living blob and sticking to it; Jesse's rib cage bent around and cracked into place about her, giving the fleshy mass support. The leg bones coiled like serpents, entrapping her thighs and calves, and holding together his quad muscles as they pulsed around her upper legs. Within seconds she was almost completely encased in dripping flesh. Jesse's vertebrae poked out as his spine ran the length of her pelvis, belly, and chest, all of them covered by his oozing cadaver, turned inside out.

The only opening that remained was over one of her eyes. Her screams were muffled, and that one eye roved about wildly.

Devon stood in front of her, dripping in gunk.

"I gotta tell ya, it is hard to breathe in there."

He reached forward and with his thumb he smoothed a portion of Jesse's inverted skull to cover up the eyehole Mandy peered out of. All that could be seen now was a lumpy form in the vague shape of a person, made up of twisted sinew, bone, and veins.

It was over so quickly, no one had time to react. Devon turned to the others.

"I was saving that for the assembly, but oh well. So"—he clapped—"who's next?"

Chad charged him, but not fast enough. Devon dropped to his knees and, pressing his palms to the concrete floor, he sank into it and out of view. Troy looked ready to punch the floor, but Chad held him back.

"He'll pay," Chad assured him, "but we've got to help Mandy and Gibbie first."

Devon's hand burst up from the floor and grabbed Chad by the ankle.

He squealed, desperately trying to yank himself free. Devon began pulling him down. Chad's heel sunk into concrete, its feel cold and clammy.

"So you think you can dance?" Chad shouted, claws slashing

deep into Devon's forearm. There was a muffled groan and the entire room shook, but the fingers released Chad and disappeared within the ground.

Gibbie moaned and Troy knelt beside him.

"Hang in there, buddy."

Chad tried helping Mandy, pulling and slashing at what was left of Jesse.

"This stuff's harder than rock!" he said.

He came and squatted next to Troy and Gibbie.

"Hey there, little man, any chance of your super strength saving the day?"

Gibbie's eyes fluttered open. He smiled drowsily at Chad.

"You're pretty," he said, and his eyes fell shut.

"Guess not," Chad said. "Maybe if we..."

His words were cut off.

"Behind you!" Troy warned, but it was too late.

A steel coil flew through the air and wrapped itself around Chad's throat. It squeezed tight and yanked him backwards, dragging him across the floor, out of the hole in the wall and into the weightlifting room.

He was lifted off the ground with a snap, and stopped with a jolt, hanging from what was left of the weightlifting machine Gibbie had trashed earlier. Chad's eyes rolled in their sockets. He looked up and Devon crouched atop the machine, leering down at him. His power over matter was growing.

"Feel the burn," the black-haired youth taunted.

He hopped off, leaving Chad hanging there like a piece of meat.

The blond gazed about frantically, his toes barely touching the ground and his gasping lungs struggling to catch a breath. The metal cord strangling him looped over a pulley, and then down to a stack of weights. The pin was pushed into the bottom plate, which meant the entire stack was what held him aloft.

He reached desperately for the metal pin. If he could pull it free...

"Nice try," Devon smirked, reaching for the weight pin himself.

Troy came at him and Devon spun about, fingers at the ready.

"Don't!" Chad gasped between struggling breaths. "His hands!"

"It's good advice," Devon added, crouching down and touching the pin. It writhed and melded into place. Chad's face was turning a deep red, and his cheeks puffed in and out. Spit bubbled over his lips with every gasping breath.

"You don't have to do this," Troy said.

"I *want* to do this," Devon replied.

"Part of you does," Troy agreed.

"Right, you can feel emotions," Devon said. "Fag."

Troy looked at the skimpy silver panties Devon had squeezed Chad into, but let it go. The cheerleader's face was turning purple. He heaved and managed to lift the weight up half-an-inch, giving Chad a chance to catch his breath, but he couldn't hold it. There was a clang and he sputtered once more.

"I know Liza's in a lot of pain," Troy said.

Devon finally noticed her, and for a moment a haze lifted from him. Troy stood between the two of them, just as Devon stood between him and Chad.

"Just try and stop me," Devon dared, wiggling his fingers.

Troy stood back. They circled each other. Devon knelt next to Liza; Troy gripped the cable choking Chad. Between the two of them they were able to ease the weight from his windpipe.

"Thanks," he gasped.

They watched as Devon knelt beside Liza.

"It's okay, baby," he murmured.

He touched the bandages around her throat and they recoiled off of her as if they were alive.

"What did he do to you?" he asked, his voice shaking.

"I cut her vocal cords," Chad snapped.

"You sure this is the time to be digging it in?" Troy asked, grimacing as he helped keep the weight off Chad's windpipe.

Under Devon's angry glare, Chad whispered, "Having second thoughts."

Devon moved his hands over Liza's bleeding throat. Under his touch her skin smeared over the wound and in moments the bleeding stopped.

"Now for the internal damage," Devon said.

His fingers pressed against her neck and, as if her flesh were heated wax, the digits sank into her. He wriggled them for a few moments. She gasped and jerked up into a sitting position. He pulled his fingers free.

"How does that feel?" he asked.

She nodded, patting her chest.

"Better, much better," she said, her voice as good as new.

"Oh crap," Chad murmured.

She smiled at Devon adoringly.

"I strung up the twinky trash who did this to you," he said, flicking his hair in Chad's direction. "Saved him for you to finish off."

She looked at Troy and Chad, her face a sour glare.

"Nice knowing you boys," Devon said, pulling a pair of earplugs from his pocket and wedging them into place. He then covered his ears with his hands and hunched down behind her.

Taking a deep breath, Liza unleashed her scream of death.

Chapter 31

"Die motherfrakkers," Liza yelled. "*Diiiiiiieeeee!*"

A high-pitched wail rose out of her, shaking the room.

"*Diiiiiiieeeee!*"

Chad instinctively buried his head into Troy's chest, and Troy held him tight, shielding him as best he could. The vibrations penetrated them. Their temples throbbed and bodies trembled. They both were whimpering in pain, their knees shaking. They tried plugging their ears, but they were directly in her line of fire.

"*Diiiiiiieeeee!*"

A trickle of blood formed in their ears, droplets running down the sides of their necks.

"*Diiiiiiieeeee!*"

The shriek built in their skulls, a hammering pressure within their fragile shells, and they knew they were about to explode. Even Devon, with his earplugs and hiding behind her, was gritting his teeth.

This was it, the sound of death.

And with a warbling croak, death went silent.

Troy and Chad remained frozen as statues, pressed against

each other. A few seconds passed. They still weren't dead. The sound of a dripping tap was the only sound in the room.

They slowly opened their eyes, bracing themselves, for surely this was a trick.

Liza panted and scowled at them. Devon looked at her questioningly, still pressing his hands to his ears.

"*Die!*" she screamed again, "*diiiiieee...*"

Troy and Chad pressed together once more for this, their final moment of life.

"*...iiiiiieeeee...*"

"I love you, Chad!" Troy cried.

"I love you too!" Chad called back.

An instant later, all they could do was whimper under Liza's onslaught. Their skulls felt ready to burst, until...

There was a catch in Liza's throat, like a clutch grinding between gears. Her cry snapped back inside of her and she grasped her throat as if she'd swallowed a stinging bee. The room fell silent.

Panting and shaking, Chad and Troy blinked repeatedly in a pained daze. They looked to each other, then to her, and slowly straightened, both of them carefully holding on to the cord around Chad's neck.

"Is that it?" Chad asked.

"*Di...*" Liza began, but a coughing fit doubled her over.

She looked to Devon in confusion.

"What's wrong with me?"

"I...I don't know," he replied. "I reconnected everything as best I could."

"As best you could?" she rasped, sounding like Kathleen Turner with a cold.

There was anger in her voice, and fear, and desperation. Beneath that Troy could feel something more, elusive yet powerful, the emotion that whipped all her other feelings into a frenzy.

I can feel her, he thought, *but what is she feeling?*

Troy carefully opened the door in his head.

"Fix me!" she demanded, grabbing Devon by the collar of his black shirt.

Troy looked to Chad, and the jock knew what drove her to desperation.

"She loves you," Troy said to Devon.

Devon glared at him.

"Of course she loves me."

Troy's brain worked frantically. He could feel Mandy growing weaker inside her prison of human flesh. Blood pooled around Gibbie's cracked head. The weight he and Chad held dropped a notch in their weakening grip, making Chad gurgle for air.

"She's afraid," Troy added, "that you're not going to love her anymore, not as she is now, not without her voice."

He was ad libbing, of course. He knew what she felt, not why—that was anybody's guess. So Troy guessed.

Liza's face blanched at his words, and the panic that he sensed pelting off her in waves told Troy that if she hadn't previously been afraid of Devon losing interest in her with her power gone, she most definitely was now. The doubt in Devon's face only made it worse. One did not have to be an empath to sense it.

"Tell her that you love her," Troy said. "It's what she wants to hear."

"Bite me," she said in her dry and brittle voice. Yet tears bubbled in her eyes.

"Please," she begged Devon, "fix me."

"Just tell her that you love her," Troy insisted.

"I..." Devon looked to her, to Troy, back to her.

"You have a choice," Troy insisted.

And Devon made it.

"Don't worry, babe," he said, "I'm going to make it all better."

He looked up at the poster of the human anatomy, and then back to her. He pressed his fingers into her throat, and they sank into her flesh. She smiled, closing her eyes, her face filled with peaceful rapture.

"I love having you inside of me," she said.

"Don't talk," he cautioned. The sweat stood out on his forehead. "Almost done. There, that should..."

Her eyes popped open, cheeks trembling.

"Liza?" Devon asked, his voice wavering.

She tried to talk, but nothing came out. She coughed, and spurts of blood hit Devon in the face. His fingers were still in her throat. His breathing quickened.

"Don't move, baby," he said. He choked back a muffled sob. "I can fix this."

His fingers moved inside of her. He bit his lip in concentration. He wiped his forehead on his sleeve. She inhaled suddenly and then stopped, her entire body going stiff. Her eyes bulged in panic. She tried to push the air back out again. Her mouth shaped the same word her victims had uttered to her.

Please.

"Hold on!" Devon begged.

He sank the fingers of his other hand into her throat.

"I can unblock it, I just..."

Minutes passed, quiet except for Devon's panting. Liza's face turned a shade of blue. Her body went limp. Her exhale never came.

"Liza?" Devon called. "Liza!"

He pressed his ear to her chest.

"Liza!"

Her torso hung from his fingertips, still deep in her neck. He lowered her to the ground and slid his fingers free.

"She's dead," he sighed.

She stared vacantly at the ceiling. A clock's hand ticked. He calmly closed her empty gaze. Devon felt very far away. It was a sensation Troy knew all too well.

"You're in shock," he said. "It's natural…"

Devon regarded him.

"I'm going to kill myself now. But first, I'm going to kill your little boyfriend"— he stared at Chad meaningfully. "Then, Troy, I'm going to kill you. Then the rest of the school. Then your parents."

Devon got off his knees and walked calmly towards Troy, hands outstretched. Troy stayed protectively in front of Chad, but the cheerleader shoved him away. The weight that was strangling the blond pulled him back onto his tiptoes.

Devon grabbed Chad's hair and yanked it back. He gave the stud muffin's neck a long lick.

"I may not be able to put people back together very well, but I'm going to take you apart bit by bit, starting with that beautiful layer of skin of yours."

Troy circled around from behind and grabbed Devon's wrists. With a forceful jerk the former wrestler yanked the black-haired teen off Chad, and tossed the boy to the ground. Devon tried to get up, but grunted as Troy landed on top of him, pinning him to the ground.

"You want to be with him so much?" Devon struggled under the weight, his arms stuck under Troy's knees, unable to touch him. "Then let me up. I'll make the two of you inseparable."

"It doesn't have to go like this," Troy said. "You can still free Chad and Mandy. We can get Gibbie to a hospital."

"And then what?" Devon laughed, a little hysterically. "We'll all be super best friends, and go to the prom together in a rented limo, and then after we graduate from college we can all buy houses on the same street and all our kids can go to the same frigging Montessori school?"

"I wasn't really thinking that far ahead," Troy admitted.

"Of course you weren't," Devon sputtered. "Why would you? High school's great for guys like you, so you just assume that whatever life brings, it'll be great too. Well, not all of us can be good little zombies."

"So that's why you did it?" Troy demanded. "That's why you killed my best friend?"

"I've killed lots of people," Devon bragged. "But Jesse, he killed himself."

"You sent him that video. You and Liza. If you hadn't..."

"Then what?" Devon sputtered. "He'd be with you?"

"He'd be alive," Troy replied.

"The alive are dead," Devon said with a maniacal titter. "It's the undead who are truly alive."

Troy released his hold on Devon and stepped back.

"What are you doing?" Devon asked, still lying on the ground and looking back over his shoulder suspiciously.

"You're hiding," Troy said, "from what you did."

"I told you, Jesse killed himself."

"You helped. And...*you* killed Liza."

Devon looked over at her.

"Chad killed her," Devon growled.

"Chad gave you a choice. You'd rather she be dead than be back the way she was."

Devon struggled for a reply. Troy was buffeted by the smaller teen's anger, fear, and sadness.

"I know how you feel," Troy continued, "and not just because I *know* how you feel."

"That's a laugh," Devon said, getting to his feet, "coming from Mr. Aberbombie football star."

"And wrestling," Troy added.

"I can kill you, you know. I've done it before, to guys just like you."

"Did it make you feel better?"

"A little," Devon nodded.

"Did it make you feel better emailing that video to Jesse?"

"Definitely."

"And when Jesse killed himself?"

"Like there was justice after all."

"He lived a lie, every day," Troy said. "Wasn't that punishment enough?"

"Not when he got to collect the social rewards, something you know all about."

"I know that I'm not willing to do it anymore," Troy said.

"If this is your coming-out speech, you can save it," Devon sneered. "I can see the headlines already. Local high-school sports hero leaves closet behind. You'll probably get a civic award. And then you'll graduate, go to the big city, party with some of the hottest guys around. You'll meet 'the one,' some Tarzan himbo who takes you away from 'the scene,' except for the occasional orgy on a gay cruise. Otherwise, the two of you'll go antiquing on Sundays after an eggs Benedict brunch, get married, rent a woman's womb for the egg you've had artificially inseminated, then hire a nanny to raise the wailing parasite. Yeah, I've read *Out* magazine. Blah, cliché, blah. Well screw that, and screw you."

Devon shoved his hands deep into the concrete floor. Tendrils of cement burst upwards, coiling like snakes around Troy's arms and shoulders, dragging him into a prostrate position, forearms to the ground, chest pressed against his hands, knees digging into concrete. He grunted and struggled futilely.

He could feel Devon's rage pounding into him, but underneath was something else as well. And that's when Troy stopped struggling.

Let him in, he told himself.

Troy closed his eyes, and thought of Jesse. They had met on the playground in Grade 2. It was overcast. Troy had forgotten his lunch.

"Here," Jesse had said, offering Troy half his Hostess cupcake. They'd been best buds ever since.

Tears bubbled in Troy's eyes.

"He's gone," Troy murmured, "he's really gone."

The stabbing in his heart was unlike any he'd ever known. It welled up inside of him and came out a lonely sob.

"Yeah, you cry, big man," Devon mocked.

Troy barely heard.

Another memory, of Jesse and him in Grade 5, sword-fighting with sticks on the top of the monkey bars at the park, of Troy pushing Jesse, Jesse falling, onto his arm, a sickening crack; and then, sitting in the emergency room, more scared than ever, for his friend, for what he'd done to him.

Jesse never told on him, and made sure Troy was the first to sign his cast.

Devon took Troy's face in his hands. The jock shook and sobbed.

More memories. Buying their first porn mags. Playing video games. Planning spring break. Never feeling alone as long as he could just hear Jesse's voice on the phone.

"Don't worry, you and Jesse will be together soon enough," Devon promised. His fingers slowly began to sink into Troy's face.

There was a clang and moan of metal as Chad violently tried to free himself, but Troy didn't struggle. He gazed full into his attacker's eyes, and let Devon feel what he felt. The pain of loss ripped through Troy, and into Devon, sending him stumbling backwards, his fingers popping free of Troy's cheeks.

"What are you doing to me?" Devon gasped. He doubled over and gripped his stomach.

Troy said nothing. He was remembering. It was near the end of summer. Jesse and Troy lay on his bed. Jesse read *The Tommy-knockers*. Troy read *The Gunslinger*. Both Stephen King novels. It was warm out. Jesse took his shirt off. Troy stared at his friend's body, the heat making him trance out. That was the moment Troy knew what he was.

Another sob rose up from Troy.

The concrete coils twisted around him were cold, cold like a body left in the ground to rot. The memories, painful as they were, the memories warmed him, so he let them fly free.

Tears welled in Devon's eyes.

"Stop it!" he shouted, the salty drops lancing the sides of his mouth. He pushed his fingers into the concrete. "I said stop it!"

The tendrils around Troy tightened. He grimaced, and as he did, so did Devon.

"Feels a bit tight, doesn't it?" Troy asked with a muffled laugh, the grief putting him on the edge of hysteria. "What you do to me, you will feel yourself."

Devon shook his head.

"I'll kill you."

The tendrils constricted like a python. Troy screamed. Devon screamed. The tendrils relaxed. Devon was panting now.

"Let's see you hurt me without a brain," Devon threatened.

He stepped towards Troy, arms outstretched.

Troy closed his eyes, and opened his heart. Before things went so wrong, Troy lay in Jesse's arms, back when they could pretend it was just a brotherly cuddle. It had been...

"...safe," Devon whispered.

He pushed tears from his eyes as he recalled Liza's embrace. He remembered holding her, and the ever-present anger and pain and loneliness would dissolve. He'd forget for a moment how much the world sucked. He would forget everything but her. And now she was dead, and he was the one who'd killed her. The realization was like a stake in his heart. He could still feel his fingers inside of her as she gasped for air.

"I killed her," he said, and the words were spinning blades dicing his insides.

"Please," Devon whimpered, the pain of losing her making him fall to his knees. He hugged himself tightly. "Make it go away," he begged of Troy.

Devon pressed his fingers into the concrete and the bindings around Troy receded into the floor.

"I let you go," he said, digging his nails into his arms as he curled into a ball. "I'll let your friends go. Just please, make this feeling stop!"

A strangled sob made him choke. He rocked himself from side to side.

"I can't," Troy said, standing over Devon. "These feelings are yours to feel."

"No," Devon gasped, clawing at his face. "I've done things...you don't even know...felt nothing but pride and..."

Troy grabbed the younger boy's wrists.

"Look at her," he ordered.

"I don't want..."

"Look at her!" Troy ordered.

Devon obeyed, staring at Liza's motionless body.

"I tried to help her," Devon said. "I tried to fix her... I... I... I killed her," he sobbed.

Troy kneeled next to him and hugged him tight.

"How can I live with this feeling?" Devon asked, pressing himself into Troy.

"Don't fight it," Troy said. "Let it wash through you."

"I can't," Devon replied, shaking his head. "It's too much. It's too frigging much. It hurts so bad."

He ripped at his chest. His body trembled uncontrollably, and his nails dug deeper, leaving bloody trenches as he scooped out troughs of skin, as if his own body were made from soft clay.

"Stop it!" Troy said, trying to grab the smaller boy's wrists.

In a burst of strength Devon pushed him away.

"I can't live with this. Not this. Not alone. Not again."

His fingers slid into his own chest as if it were pudding. He was in past his wrist. Troy watched the muscles in Devon's forearm clench. The younger boy's face spasmed and his arm made a jerky tug. His face relaxed, peaceful, as his body collapsed to the floor.

In his hand, he held his own heart.

Epilogue

There was a great whining of metal that ended in a twanging snap and the clatter of dropping weights. Chad fell to his hands and knees, gasping. With a final burst of strength he'd finally managed to break the metal cord that was killing him and he quickly un-coiled it from around his throat.

"Mandy," he said between panting breaths.

He and Troy turned to the glob that was all that was left of Jesse, which had now become Mandy's coffin. Chad got up, claws extended.

"I'm coming for you, baby," he said, but Troy held him back by the shoulder, pointing to Mandy's prison. It began to vibrate.

"I don't think she needs us to rescue her," Troy said. "In fact, we might want to take..."

The glob exploded outward. Pieces smacked into Troy and Chad.

Mandy stood there, her dress stuck to her sweat-covered body, fingers squeezed into a pair of fists.

"All right, it's on," she said, eyes blinking in the sudden light as she searched for Devon.

Her eyes fell on him. He clasped his heart.

"Oh," she said, her face squelching in revulsion. "Sick."

"You made your force field expand outwards," a meek voice said from behind them all.

"Gibbie!" Troy said, and they all rushed to the geeky boy's side. "You okay?"

"A little woozy," he answered.

"It's all right, buddy," Troy said, picking him up. "We're going to get you to a hospital, okay?"

"Okay," Gibbie said.

Troy carried him to the door, still locked. Gibbie gave it a shove and it flew off its hinges. They walked through the empty gym, down the school's deserted halls. They got to the front door, and from there heard the crackle of a speaker in the auditorium.

"We are gathered here today to honor, and say goodbye to, one of our own."

It was Coach Lenwick who spoke.

Troy looked towards the memorial longingly.

"It's okay," Mandy said. She took Gibbie's arm and put it around her shoulder.

"I can stand," he said to Troy, and he set his younger brother down.

"I'll take him to emergency," Mandy said.

Still, Troy hesitated.

"He was your best friend," Chad said, "and more. You should be in there."

Troy nodded.

"Thanks, guys," he said. There were tears in his eyes.

He opened the auditorium doors and, with a final look at the others (Gibbie gave him a thumbs-up), walked in.

"You coming?" Mandy asked Chad. He still wore only the pair of silver Speedos.

"I think I'd like to hear this," he answered, standing on tiptoe so he could see through the window in the auditorium door.

"Well, buddy," she said to Gibbie, "I guess it's just you and me."

"Chad," Gibbie said.

"Yeah," he replied.

"Before we go, could I just...could I have one kiss?"

Chad looked at his bedraggled form.

"Yeah, I think I can set that up."

He came over, intending to just give Gibbie a peck on the lips, but as he leaned in and saw Gibbie's big eyes behind his thick glasses, he knew better. He could never love Gibbie the way he deserved to be loved, but as their lips met, he nibbled, and even gave the small boy a flick of tongue.

"Thanks," Gibbie said, a dreamily content look on his face.

"No problem," Chad replied.

"And here." He pulled out the Barbie journal from his satchel and handed it to Chad. "I guess you might want this back."

Chad took it, a quizzical look on his face.

"Uh, this isn't mine."

"Yeah right," Mandy scoffed. But a moment later, "Oh my God, you're not kidding. Well then, whose is it?"

They all looked back to the auditorium, to where Troy was getting up onstage.

"Well I'll be," Mandy murmured. "That boy is just full of surprises."

She turned and gently led Gibbie towards the door. "Let's get you stitched up."

Chad looked down at Troy's Barbie journal, and propped the door open a bit so he could hear the jock's speech.

"I suppose you're wondering why I look like such a mess," Troy said to his schoolmates and teachers. He gazed down at himself, at his ripped suit covered in bits of what was left of Jesse.

"Like the walking dead," Chad said, wiping a bit of Jesse off himself.

The crowd murmured and the staff kept exchanging worried glances. Principal McGee mopped his forehead with a handkerchief. Coach Lenwick was stone-faced, but gave Troy an encouraging nod. At the very back of the room, from behind a door opened a smidge, Chad hugged himself nervously.

"I could get into it," Troy continued, "but the truth is we're not here to talk about me. We're here to talk about Jesse, his life, his loves."

He gazed upon the crowd, then down at the cue cards he'd prepared, and then back up at the crowd. He sighed and turned the cue cards face down.

"I sense a lot of emotion out there. Sadness. Disbelief. Even some anger. According to the grief counselors, anger is to be expected. It's like we've been abandoned by one we love."

He took a deep breath.

"But there's something they've left out, something no one wants to talk about. Jesse killed himself. We all know it, and we all pretend to want to know why. Well, here it is. My best friend hanged himself after he was sent a video of him and another guy being intimate together."

There were murmurs in the crowd.

"It's been in the papers now, but still no one thinks I should be talking about it here. You're thinking, that's not how Jesse would want to be remembered. Or, he was set up. It's that other guy's fault. But I can't help but look out at this crowd and wonder, what if Jesse had not killed himself? What if, after that video got out, he'd showed up at school the next day? What if he showed up holding that other guy's hand? I won't ever get an answer, not for sure, but whatever Jesse imagined happening, he pictured your faces, the faces I'm looking into right now. He feared you all so much that he'd rather die than face you as himself. This is a guy who squared off against linebackers on steroids without blinking.

But he couldn't face you. You want to know who that other person in the video was? It was me. I loved him as a friend, and as more than a friend."

There was a rustle of shock running through the crowd. At the back of the auditorium, Chad felt salty tears dribble down his cheeks. Jesse's mom and dad sat in the front row. She gripped her mouth and her husband put his arm around her shoulder, glaring at Troy.

"That's enough," the principal said under his breath, appearing ready to storm forward. Chad's dad grabbed him and held him back.

"Let him finish."

The principal looked ready to argue. The coach outweighed him by eighty pounds of pure muscle.

"I said," the coach repeated in a stony voice, towering over his boss, "let him finish."

"I'm sorry," Troy said, "I'm not trying to be dramatic, but if we're going to remember Jesse, then we're going to remember him for more than the mask he felt he had to wear every day so that he could pass as someone he knew you would like, and admire, and look up to. He made the decision to end his life. Him, and only him. But each of us killed him in a million little ways. When the guys on the football team would call each other 'fag.' When we picked on anyone who didn't quite fit in. When we stuck to our own little cliques. We've all done it, but maybe if we'd done it a little bit less, he'd still be here."

He thought of Liza and Devon. Had they been driven to this?

"Suicide isn't an answer..."

Or murder.

"We have to remember that, and we have to be better for each other."

He paused, and took a deep breath.

"I love you, Jesse, and I miss you very much."

At first no one reacted.

Chad stepped forward, in his little silver Speedo, clapping loudly. Everyone turned and stared, and for a moment his father looked like he wanted to crumble into dust. But, hardening his face, Coach Lenwick began clapping in time with his son.

Markham stood up and jerked Riley up with him. Riley glared at the rest of the football team, and soon Troy was receiving a standing ovation.

Jesse's mom cried harder than anyone, but she too struggled to her feet.

Only his dad remained seated, and Troy felt the waves of hatred buffeting off him. It was then Troy wondered if it really was the kids at school that Jesse was most afraid of facing.

"So now what?" Chad asked hours later as he drove Troy home.

Chad wore Troy's suit jacket.

"Go to school tomorrow, I guess," Troy replied. "Unlike Jesse, they're going to have to deal with me."

There were, however, several loose ends Troy, Chad, Mandy, and Gibbie had to tie up. Gibbie had suffered a cracked skull, but no concussion, and after the doctors patched him up it was he who carried Devon and Liza's bodies to Mandy's car. Many people would have seen them, which is where Mandy came in handy.

Gibbie and Chad dug the graves in an isolated field a few miles outside of town. There was no one to report either Liza or Devon missing, and the pair might have faded in the town's memory, revived occasionally during conversations of "whatever happened to...?" except for the many twisted bodies later discovered in Mrs. Dedarling's mansion—including what was left of Mrs. Dedarling, and Liza's ex-boyfriend.

Devon became the prime suspect and the focus of an entire

episode of *America's Most Wanted.*

Falsifying a certificate that said Jesse's remains had been cremated by mistake was a little trickier, but Mandy managed to filch the necessary paperwork from the crematorium. It was Troy who delivered the remains to Jesse's parents. His dad slammed down the newspaper and left the room as soon as he saw Troy at the door, but Jesse's mom gave Troy a big hug.

"You are very brave," she said to him, "and I wish our son had told us he was gay. I wished we'd been better parents."

Troy nodded.

"I know how you feel. The words 'if only' keep running through my head."

There came a squeak of floorboards and Troy tensed, readying to face Jesse's father. But it was not Jesse's dad who walked into the living room. For just a moment, Troy thought it was Jesse himself. Troy flinched, thinking Devon had somehow survived, and had come for one final battle. But in flashes of detail, Troy noticed this guy was just a bit taller than Jesse, the face a nod prettier, the body geared more towards a runway than a football field, and whereas Jesse shaved his head, this young man had baby dreads sprouting from his scalp. He also wore a bright pink button-down made from silk that Jesse would have handed over to his girlfriend.

"Hey, Troy, it's been a while," the young man said.

"Felix?" Troy gaped at Jesse's older brother. "I saw you in that Calvin Klein ad a few months back, but I still didn't quite believe..."

Felix shrugged, but his smile bathed in the compliment.

"What can I say? College has been good to me."

Real good, Troy thought.

"Thanks," Felix said, though Troy was certain he'd kept his mouth closed. "Is that..." Felix pointed to the package under Troy's arm.

"Yes," Troy coughed.

He handed Jesse's remains to his mom. Staring at the box, Troy felt his own throat constrict. It was Mandy, Gibbie, and Chad who'd scraped up what was left of the football captain's body, and it was Mandy who'd sweet-talked the 40-year-old deadbeat at the crematorium into burning it.

Jesse's mom's face grew somber.

"I should sue them for cremating him by mistake."

Troy gave her an empathic nudge.

She sighed, "But now I can keep him on the mantle. The thought of him, cold in the ground, all alone..."

She shuddered. Felix put his arm around her and she patted his hand.

"Felix, if you wouldn't mind showing Troy out," she said, giving Troy a final hug before leaving the room.

At the door, Felix said, "I want to thank you for speaking up, about who my brother really was. You've got a pretty big pair on you, for a white guy."

Troy nodded. "Not sure that your dad feels the same way."

"Yeah," Felix snorted, "and he sure as hell wasn't happy when your speech inspired me to come out."

"You're..."

"Pink mafia," he smiled, and Troy felt an electric exchange of sexual chemistry. Reluctantly, he forced it into the room in his head.

"Well, take it easy, man," Felix said, and Troy was disappointed by the handshake they shared instead of a hug. "And if you ever feel like checking out the college campus in Calebraton, come visit me. I'll introduce you to the guys at my gayternity."

"Gay fraternity?" Troy inquired.

Felix winked. "I get the feeling you'd fit right in."

And so everything was put in order, neat and tidy as could be.

Instead of being reviled, as he assumed he would be after his speech, by the next semester Troy found himself volunteering as a peer counselor at school. Being an empath had its advantages. Even Markham and Riley came to him for advice.

"So, since we like hanging out with each other more than with girls, does that make us gay?" Markham asked.

"I'm going to get back to you on that one," Troy replied, veering away from them and coming up to Chad. He gave the blond a kiss on the lips. They held hands on the way to the cafeteria.

"I have something for you," Chad said as they sat down with their trays of mystery meat and lumpy potatoes.

"Here," Chad said, handing a wrapped package to Troy.

"It's not my birthday," he said, ripping it open. He smiled and held up the Paris Hilton *Heiress Diary: Confess It All to Me.*

"Nice," Troy smiled.

Mandy sat next to them. Her hair had grown back, but she still wore the nose ring.

"You know, this Virginia Woolf chick had some wacky ideas," she said, setting down the book *To the Lighthouse*. To Troy she added, "Nice journal."

"My boyfriend gave it to me," Troy bragged.

Gibbie tittered as he sat down with them.

"You are never going to believe who's going to be at the *Star Trek* convention next month. Patrick Stewart!"

"Jean-Luc Picard?" Mandy asked. "He's pretty sexy for an older guy."

Chad and Troy looked at her in surprise.

"I told you before, it's not geeky to like *The Next Generation*," she said defensively. "And I bet if you guys gave *Deep Space Nine* a chance, you'd find the war between the Federation and the Dominion to be pretty addictive."

Troy made a "W" with the thumbs and pointing fingers of his two hands.

"Show them what I got you," Chad said excitedly.

"Hey, Paris Hilton!" Gibbie said, eyeing the journal. "Are we all on for the season premiere of *The Simple Life: Battle of the Bulge*? I hear Paris and Nicole have to wear fat suits the entire season."

"I'll bring the popcorn," Mandy said, giving him a high-five. As she picked at her mashed potatoes she said to Troy, "I still don't get why you have to write in little girl journals."

"I told you, when I was a kid I was a little emotionally repressed," Troy said.

"A little?" Gibbie asked.

"When you were a kid?" Chad added.

"So my dad suggested I write down my feelings," Troy elaborated. "I told him I didn't have any, so he asked me who was the most emotional person in the world that I could think of."

"He said me," Chad bragged. "He punched me in Grade 3 and I bawled for hours. I was a very expressive child."

"You know, I think that's the only time I ever got sent to the corner," Troy mused. "Anyway, whenever I was feeling a little too shut down or on the verge of punching someone, I'd channel my inner Chad and write in my journal in his voice. I really don't see why you're all making such a big deal out of this."

"The big deal is I don't dot my I's with little hearts," Chad replied.

"How come Dad never gave me a journal?" Gibbie asked.

"Dude, you lucked out on not having to do all sorts of New Age crap thanks to me."

Troy sipped on his protein shake, opening the journal. A smile creased his handsome features.

"Baby," he said, "you even wrote me a little note in here."

Chad shook his head.

"No I didn't."

Leaning over, he cursed. "No wonder it was on sale. Some jerk wad's already written in it."

"Wait." Troy held up his hand. "*Queeroes*," he read out loud. "*They know who you are, and they know what you can do. They came for us. Now they're coming for you.*"

The cafeteria lights flickered. The sky beyond the windows darkened. A rumble of thunder rattled the air. They looked to each other with growing worry.

"This better not screw up prom," Mandy snapped, " 'cause Markham *so* just asked me out."

~